Charter and Supplements of the Pennsylvania Railroad Company

Anatiposi

Anonymous

Charter and Supplements of the Pennsylvania Railroad Company

Reprint of the original, first published in 1859.

1st Edition 2023 | ISBN: 978-3-38230-734-9

Anatiposi Verlag is an imprint of Outlook Verlagsgesellschaft mbH.

Verlag (Publisher): Outlook Verlag GmbH, Zeilweg 44, 60439 Frankfurt, Deutschland
Vertretungsberechtigt (Authorized to represent): E. Roepke, Zeilweg 44, 60439 Frankfurt, Deutschland
Druck (Print): Books on Demand GmbH, In de Tarpen 42, 22848 Norderstedt, Deutschland

CHARTER AND SUPPLEMENTS

OF THE

Pennsylvania Railroad Company,

WITH THE

ACTS OF ASSEMBLY AND MUNICIPAL ORDINANCES

AFFECTING THE COMPANY;

TOGETHER WITH THE

BY-LAWS OF THE BOARD OF DIRECTORS.

PHILADELPHIA:
1859.

CONTENTS.

CHARTER

OF THE

PENNSYLVANIA RAILROAD COMPANY,

WITH ITS SUPPLEMENTS, &c.

AN ACT

TO INCORPORATE THE

PENNSYLVANIA RAILROAD COMPANY.

SECTION 1. That Thomas P. Cope, Robert Toland, William M. Meredith, A. S. Roberts, John K. Kane, John B. Myers, Henry Welsh, John M. Atwood, Henry D. Gilpin, John A. Brown, George Cadwalader, Thomas M. Petit, George W. Toland, A. J. Lewis, A. G. Ralston, David S. Brown, William C. Patterson, Henry White, James Magee, Hugh Campbell, Henry M. Watts, Gideon Scull, Charles S. Wood, J. Fisher Leaming, Thomas C. Rockhill, Thomas P. Hoopes, Robert Allen, Alexander Fullerton, John Welsh, junior, Alexander Osbourn, William Reynolds, William S. Charnley, B. M. Hinchman, Townsend Sharpless, C. G. Childs, Charles Humphreys, Thomas Tustin, Thomas Robbins, William Musser, Robert Steen, Edward Siter, Charles Macalester, Joseph R. Evans, Edward Duff, Henry M. Phillips, Elhanan W. Keyser, Hyman Gratz, John White, John J. Ridgway, Walter R. Johnson, Elliot Cresson, Josiah Randall, J. Rhea Barton, John Swift, George Campbell, G. R. Childs, Hugh Catherwood, Horn R. Kneass, James Steel, James M. Davis, Joseph A. Clay and William P. Smith, of the city of Philadelphia; Thomas Sparks, Thomas McCully, Isaac W. Norris, George M. Stroud, George N. Baker, James Martin, E. A. Penniman, Abraham Helfenstein, Philip M. Price, John J. McCahen, George W. Carpenter, John S. Littell, Samuel C. Ford, Benjamin Crispin, Nathan Trotter, Jacob Broom, Thomas D. Grover, John Naglee, Archibald Wright, Edward F. Gay, William S. Hallowell, William English, Joseph Lippencott, Robert Flinn, Jr., Christopher Mason, John T. Smith, Charles Brown, John Miller, Michael D. Whartman, John S. Cash, Joseph Baker, Mitchell Bomeisler, Samuel Jackson, Peter Rambo, John Robbins, George Shetsline, Samuel Ovenshine, James Enew, Jr., Henry Manderfield, David F. Condie, Benjamin L. Berry, Joseph Diamond, William Laughlin, and Levi Strickland, of the county of Philadelphia; Samuel D. Ingham, of Bucks county; Joel K. Names of Commissioners.

Names of Commissioners.

Mann, Charles Kugler, of Montgomery county; H. Jones Brooke, of Delaware county; Thomas S. Bell, Francis James, Robert Parke, of Chester county; Alexander L. Hays, Emanuel C. Reigart, John N. Lane, Reah Frazer, Benjamin G. Herr, Edward Davies, Reuben Mullison, Bernard Flinn, Samuel Shoch, John F. Huston, J. S. Clarkson, Frederick Hipple, Reuben Hause, of Lancaster county; Henry Flannery, Henry W. Smith, J. Pringle Jones, Henry A. Muhlenburg, Michael K. Boyer, John S. Heister, William High, William Heidenreich, Charles Keely, J. Glancy Jones, of Berks county; Levi Kline, of Lebanon county; Valentine Hummell, senior, William Ayres, Jacob M. Haldeman, James McCormick, James Peacock, Henry Buehler, John C. Bucher, Simon Cameron, David R. Porter, of Dauphin county; Benjamin McIntyre, Robert Elliott, James McFarlane, George Stroop, Robert S. King, Findley McCowan, Hugh R. Wilson, Henry Fetter, and Jacob Keiser, of Perry county; James Mathers, Andrew Parker, of Juniata county; Abraham S. Wilson, James Criswell, Reuben C. Hale, Francis W. Rawle, Moses Montgomery, Joseph Milliken, Joseph Ard, Joseph Kyle, David Zook, and William Reed, of Mifflin county; John G. Miles, John Kerr, A. P. Wilson, Edwin F. Shoenberger, Benjamin Leas, John McCahan, John Long, Brice Blair, Thomas E. Orbeson, Edward Bell, William Williams, and John Porter, of Huntingdon county; James Irvin, James T. Hale, W. W. Houston, James Potter, Abraham S. Valentine, Henry Brokerhoff, William F. Reynolds, and Daniel Ulman, of Centre county; A. K Wright, A. B. Reed, J. W. Smith, of Clearfield county; John Linton, W. A. Smith, John Mathew, John Fenlon, Peter Livergood, Edward Shoemaker, Stephen Lloyd, and Richard Lewis, of Cambria county; James Clark, George Mulholland, Jr., David Ralston, Daniel Stanard, of Indiana county; John Hill, J. R. Logan, John M. Laird, Henry McBride, Joseph Harvey, Hugh Irwin, S. L. Carpenter, F. J. Cope, Richard Coulter, of Westmoreland county; Jesse Carothers, Joshua Hanna, Harmar Denny, Thomas Bakewell, John Bigler, William Wilkins, Wilson McCandless, William McKnight, William Eichbaum, C. McGee, William Larrimer, James Marshall, John T. Wilson, William R. Vankirk, Samuel Walker, E. Percival, Andrew Bayne, John Hay, H. G. Roland, Hiram Hultz, and Samuel W. Black, of Allegheny county; Michael Doudel, Samuel Wagner, Charles Weiser, Daniel Hartman, A. C. Ramsey, of York county; Jacob Mechling, John Bredin, of Butler county; Robert H. Hammond, Jesse C. Horton, J. M. Pollock, John Forsyth, A. Jordan, C. W. Hegins, Samuel Hepburn, and E. Greenough, of Northumberland county; Ner Middleswarth, Robert Cander, Henry Snyder, John L. Watson, and Robert Hays, of the county of Union; David Leech, Philip Klinginsmith, and Lewis Brenaman, of Armstrong county; Henry Allen, John P. McGlathery, David Norwood, Samuel Vanhorn, William Maginniss, James Stewart, James Culbertson, Joseph Pollock, and Alva Leonard, of the county of Beaver; George Chambers, Frederick Smith, and William Baker, of the county of Franklin; Thomas H. Sill, Giles Sanford, John H. Walker, C. M. Reed, C. McSparren, George Seldon, and John Galbraith, of Erie county; Joel B. Curtis, Samuel Goodman, David Cortney, R. W. Cunningham, and John Hoge, of Mercer county; Thomas Ringland, John Wishart, T. M. T. McKennon, A. W. Acheson, James Gordon, and John Grayson, of Washington county; Morrow B. Lowry, J. Porter Brawley, and Joseph Patton, of Crawford county; Abbott Green, William Cameron, Nathan Mitchel, Levi B. Christ, Joseph Casey, Henry C. Eyre, of Union county; William Donaldson, Joseph Paxton, of Columbia county, be and they are hereby appointed commissioners, to do and perform the several acts and things hereinafter mentioned, that is to say, they, or such of them as shall act in the premises, not less than twelve, shall before proceeding to the performance of their duties, be respectively sworn or affirmed before an officer competent to administer oaths, well and truly to perform the duties enjoined upon them by this act; and as soon as conveniently may be, and within three months next after the passage of this act, shall procure and open suitable books at such proper times and places as they may designate, in the cities of Philadelphia, Lancaster, and Pittsburgh, and in the boroughs of Harrisburg, Lewistown, Huntingdon, Greensburg, Bloomfield and Blairsville, and at such other places as they may deem expedient, of which times and places at least thirty days' previous public notice shall be given, in not less than three daily newspapers published in Philadelphia, and in not less than two daily or weekly papers in the other places named, if so many are therein published, in which books they shall enter as follows: "We whose names are hereunto subscribed, do promise to pay to the President, Directors, and Company of the Pennsylvania Railroad Company, the sum of fifty dollars for each and every share of stock set opposite to our respective names, in such manner and proportions, and at such times, not exceeding five dollars per share, in any period of sixty days, as shall be determined by the president and directors of said company, in pursuance of an act entitled 'An

Names of Commissioners.

Twelve commissioners necessary to act.

Subscription books to be opened at Harrisburg, Lewistown, Huntingdon, Greensburg, Bloomfield, and Blairsville, upon 30 days' notice.

Form of subscription to the stock.

Commissioners to give all persons duly qualified an opportunity to subscribe.

Who may lawfully subscribe.

Books to be open six hours a day, for 10 days, unless 150,000 shares be sooner subscribed.

Commissioners may adjourn from time to time.

Five dollars a share to be paid at the time of subscription.

If more than capital subscribed, shares to be rateably diminished.

Shares increased by sup. April 23, 1852, sec. 1, post, p. 33. Further increased by act of May 6, 1852, sec. 4, post, p. 48. Further increased by sup. May 2, 1855, sec. 1, post, p. 38, and further increased by act of May 16, 1857, sec. 3, post, p. 62.

Act to incorporate the Pennsylvania Railroad Company.' Witness our hands and seals, the day of one thousand eight hundred and ." And at the times and places so designated and named in the public notices to be given as aforesaid, the said commissioners, by themselves, or by committees to be by them appointed, shall attend and furnish to all persons duly qualified who shall offer to subscribe, an opportunity of so doing, and it shall be lawful for all such persons, and for all firms, copartnerships, and bodies politic and corporate, by themselves, or by persons duly authorized, to subscribe for shares in said stock, and the said books shall be kept open at least six hours in every juridical day for the term of ten days, unless the whole number of one hundred and fifty thousand shares shall have been sooner subscribed, and if at the expiration of ten days, the said books shall not have the whole number of shares aforesaid subscribed therein, the said commissioners may adjourn from time to time, and transfer the said books elsewhere, until the whole number of one hundred and fifty thousand shares shall have been subscribed, of which adjournments and transfers the said commissioners shall give such public notice as in their opinion the occasion may require; and when the whole number of shares before mentioned shall have been subscribed, the books shall be closed. *Provided*, That no subscription for such stock shall be valid unless the party or parties making the same shall, at the time of subscribing, pay to said commissioners five dollars on each and every share, for the use of the company. *And provided further*, That if more than one hundred and fifty thousand shares shall have been subscribed within ten days, and before the closing of the books as aforesaid, the commissioners shall reduce the subscriptions pro rata as near as practicable, in such manner as to them may appear equitable, until the number of shares do not exceed one hundred and fifty thousand, but no subscription for ten shares or under shall be so reduced.

Commissioners to certify to the governor, under qualification, the number of shares subscribed.

When 50,000 shares are subscribed, and \$5 a share paid, governor to issue letters-patent.

SECTION 2. That when fifty thousand shares or more of the said stock shall have been subscribed, and five dollars paid on each and every share as aforesaid, the said commissioners, acting in the premises as aforesaid, or a majority of them, shall certify to the governor, which certificate shall be verified by the oath or affirmation of at least two of said commissioners, the names of the subscribers and the number of shares subscribed by each, and that five dollars on each have been paid; whereupon the governor shall, by letters-patent under his hand and the seal of the commonwealth, create and constitute the subscribers, and if the subscription be not full at the time, those who shall thereafter subscribe to the number of shares aforesaid, their successors and assigns, into a body politic and corporate in deed and in law, by the name, style and title of "The Pennsylvania Railroad Company," and by the said name, style and title, the said subscribers shall have perpetual succession, with all the privileges, franchises and immunities incident to a corporation, and be able to sue and be sued, plead and be impleaded, in all courts of record and elsewhere; and to purchase, receive, have, hold, use and enjoy, to them and their successors, lands, tenements and hereditaments, engines, locomotives, cars, goods, chattels, and estate real and personal, of what kind or quality soever; and the same from time to time to sell, exchange, mortgage, grant, alien, or otherwise dispose of; and to make dividends of such portion of the profits as they may deem proper, and also to make and have a common seal, and the same to alter and renew at pleasure, and also to ordain, establish, and put in execution such by-laws, ordinances, and regulations as shall appear necessary or convenient for the government of said corporation, not being contrary to the constitution and laws of the United States, or of this commonwealth; and generally to do all and singular the matters and things which to them it shall lawfully appertain to do for the well-being of said corporation, and the due ordering and management of the affairs thereof. *Provided*, That nothing herein contained shall be so construed as in any way giving to said corporation any banking privileges whatever, or any other liberties, privileges or franchises but such as may be necessary or convenient to the procuring, owning, making, maintaining, regulating, and using said railroad, the locomotives, machinery, cars and other appendages thereof, and the conveyance of passengers, the transportation of the mail, and of goods, merchandise, commodities and things thereon. *And provided further*, That said company shall not purchase or hold any real estate except such as may be necessary or convenient for the making and constructing of said railroad, or for the furnishing of materials therefor, and for the accommodation of depots, offices, warehouses, machine-shops, toll-houses, engine and water-stations, and other appropriate appurtenances, and for the persons and things employed or used in or about the same. *Provided*, That the whole amount of debts or other liabilities of said company, including loans, shall not at any time exceed one-half of the amount of capital actually paid in. *And provided further*, That no part of the capital stock or other funds of the company shall be at any time, directly or indirectly, loaned to any director, officer, or agent of said company.

The title of the corporation to be "The Pennsylvania Railroad Company."

Ordinary franchises.

Not to be construed as including banking privileges.

To purchase and hold real estate for the making and accommodation of the railroad only.

Debts never to exceed one-half of capital paid in. By sup. 18th April, 1854, post, p. 37, authorized to increase loans, and see act of May 16, 1857, sec. 3, post, p. 62.

No loan to be made to a director, officer, or agent.

Commissioners to give 20 days' notice to organize and elect directors.

SECTION 3. The said commissioners, or a majority of them, acting in the premises as aforesaid, shall, as soon as conveniently may be after the said letters patent shall have been obtained, appoint a time and place for the subscribers to meet in order to organize the said company, and shall give at least twenty days' previous notice thereof in the various papers before mentioned, and the said subscribers, when met, shall by ballot elect, by a majority of the votes present, to be given in person or by proxy, thirteen directors, all of whom shall be citizens and residents of this Commonwealth, and shall be owners respectively of at least twenty shares in the stock of said company; the said directors and those thereafter to be chosen in pursuance of the provisions of this act, at their first meeting shall choose by ballot one of their own number as president of said company, and the said president and directors shall conduct and manage the affairs and business of said company until the first Monday of June then next ensuing, and until others are chosen, and may make, ordain, and establish such by-laws, rules, orders and regulations, and do and perform such other matters and things as are by this act authorized.

Qualifications of a director. Altered, see sec. 3, Sup. May 2, 1855, post, p. 38.

At their first meeting, the directors shall choose a president.

May elect a Vice President, see sec. 3, Sup. 23d March, 1853, post, p. 35.

President and directors shall serve until first Monday of June succeeding, and until others are chosen.

Annual meeting of stockholders to take place on first Monday of Dec., at any place designated in the by-laws, on 20 days' notice in three or more newspapers, and directors chosen.

Changed to first Monday of Feb. by 2d sec. Act 26th April, 1850; see p. 32.

Annual election of directors to first Monday of March by sec. 2, Sup. May 2, 1855, post, p. 38.

Stockholders may, at annual meeting, make, alter, or repeal the by-laws.

Stockholders may be convened by president or directors at any other time and place, in pursuance of the by-laws.

President, on request of stockholders representing one-tenth in number and interest of stock, may call a special meeting of stockholders.

Call to state the specific object of meeting, and no

SECTION 4. That the stockholders shall meet on the first Monday of December in every year, at such place in this Commonwealth as may be designated by the by-laws of the company, of which at least twenty days' previous notice shall be given in three or more daily newspapers published in the city of Philadelphia and elsewhere, as the board shall direct, and choose by a majority of votes thirteen directors, qualified as provided in the preceding section, for the year ensuing, who shall continue in office until the next annual election, and until others are chosen; at which annual meeting the said stockholders shall have full power and authority to make, alter, or repeal, by a majority of the votes given, any or all such by-laws, rules, orders, and regulations as aforesaid, and do and perform every other corporate act authorized by their charter. The stockholders may meet at such other times and places as they may be summoned by the president and directors in such manner and form, and giving such notice as may be prescribed by the by-laws; and the president, on the request, in writing, of any number of stockholders representing not less than one-tenth in number and interest, shall call a special meeting, giving the like notice, and stating specifically the objects of such meeting; and the objects stated in such notice, and no other, shall be acted upon at such meeting; nor shall any business be transacted at any such special meeting, unless a majority of the stock shall be there represented; but the meeting may adjourn from day to day, or until such times as a majority in interest shall be present.

other business shall be transacted.

SECTION 5. That the elections for directors provided for in this act, shall be conducted in the following manner, that is to say: at the first election, the commissioners shall appoint three stockholders, not being candidates, to be judges of the said election, and to hold the same; and at every succeeding election, the directors for the time being shall appoint three stockholders, who shall not be directors nor candidates, for the like purpose; and the persons so appointed by said commissioners and directors, shall respectively take and subscribe an oath or affirmation before an alderman or justice of the peace, well and truly, according to law, to conduct such election to the best of their knowledge and ability, and the said judges shall decide upon the qualifications of voters, and when the election is closed, shall count the votes and declare who have been elected; and if it shall at any time happen that an election of directors shall not be made at the time specified, the corporation shall not for that reason be dissolved, but it shall be lawful to hold and make such election of directors on any day within three months thereafter, by giving at least ten days' previous notice of the time and place of holding said election, in the newspapers aforesaid, and the directors of the preceding year shall in that case continue in office, and be invested with all powers belonging to them as such, until others are elected in their stead. In case of the death, resignation or removal from this State of a director, or a failure to elect, in case of a tie vote, or in case any one of them ceases to be qualified to act as a director in the manner hereinbefore provided, the vacancy may be filled by the board of directors. At all general meetings or elections by the stockholders, each share of stock shall entitle the holder thereof to one vote, and each ballot shall have endorsed thereon the number of shares thereby represented, but no share or shares transferred within sixty days next preceding any election or general meeting of the stockholders shall entitle the holder or holders thereof to vote at any such election or general meeting; nor shall any person or party, females excepted, residing within ten miles of the place appointed for any such election or general meeting, be entitled to vote by proxy. No person shall represent by proxy more than three absent stockholders, nor shall any proxy be received, or entitle the holder thereof to vote, unless the same shall bear date, and have been duly executed and acknowledged before some person legally authorized at the place of executing the same to take such acknowledgments, within the three months next preceding such

Mode of conducting elections of directors.

See sec. 3, Sup. May 2, 1855, post, p. 38, as to qualifications for directors.

If no election is made, another may be held within three months, on ten days' notice.

Directors to supply vacancies in their own body; also in case of a tie vote.

See sec. 3, Sup. May 2, 1855, post, 38.

Each share entitled to one vote. See 1st sec. Sup. 27th March, 1848; post, p. 26.

Shares transferred within 60 days of an election not to entitle the holder to a vote.

No one but a female, within ten miles of a general meeting, to vote by proxy.

No person shall represent by proxy more than three absent stockholders.

Proxies to be acknowledged within three

months of the election.

Proxies voted upon to be filed among the papers of the company.

election or general meeting, and every such proxy received and voted upon as aforesaid, shall be retained and filed amongst the papers of the company until after the next annual election or general meeting, subject to the inspection or examination of any stockholder who may desire it.

The powers of the corporation to be exercised by the president and directors.

Seven to form a quorum.

The president, when present, to preside.

The directors to keep fair minutes of their proceedings.

May choose secretary, treasurer, and other officers.

May require security from any of their officers or agents.

The treasurer shall not give less than $30,000 security.

The condition of the bond of the treasurer.

The bond to be renewed at least once in two years.

SECTION 6. That the president and directors for the time being are hereby authorized and empowered to exercise all the powers granted to the corporation. They shall meet at such times and places as shall be by them deemed most convenient for the transaction of their business, and when met, seven shall be a quorum; the president, if present, shall preside at all meetings of the board, and when absent, the board shall appoint a president *pro tem.* They shall keep minutes of their proceedings fairly entered in a suitable book to be kept for that purpose; they shall choose a secretary and treasurer, and may appoint or employ all such officers, engineers, agents, superintendents, artisans, workmen, or other persons, as in their opinion may be necessary or proper in the conducting and management of the affairs and business of said corporation, at such times, in such manner, and under such regulations as they may from time to time determine; they may require security in such amounts as they may deem necessary, of each or any of said officers or other persons by them appointed or employed, and generally to do all other such acts, matters, and things, as by this act and the by-laws and regulations of the said company they may be authorized to do. The treasurer of said company shall enter into one or more sureties, satisfactory to the president and directors, in a sum not less than thirty thousand dollars, conditioned for the faithful discharge of all the duties of his office while he shall continue to hold the same, and for faithfully accounting for and paying over according to law and the by-laws of the company, all moneys that may come into his hands as treasurer aforesaid, and for the payment to his successor in office, or other person authorized by the president and directors to receive the same, the balance of all such moneys, and in like manner for the delivery to said successor, or other person authorized as aforesaid, all books, papers, documents, accounts and property that he may have or hold by virtue of his office, and the bond or bonds of the treasurer shall be renewed at least once in every two years.

Salaries and wages.

No director to be allowed compensation but the president.

SECTION 7. The president and directors shall fix the amount of salaries and wages of the several officers, engineers, and agents employed by them, but no director shall be allowed any compensation but the president, whose salary shall be fixed by the vote of a majority of all the directors.

Certificates of stock to be delivered to the stockholders.

How to be signed, countersigned and sealed.

Stock transferable at pleasure in the presence of the president or treasurer.

The transferee of stock to be a member of the corporation.

No certificate of stock not paid for, to be transferred without the consent of the directors.

SECTION 8. That the president and directors first chosen shall procure certificates or evidences of stock for all the shares of the said company, and shall deliver one or more certificates or evidences, signed by the president and countersigned by the treasurer, and sealed with the common seal of the corporation, to each person or party entitled to receive the same, according to the number of shares by him, her, or them, respectively subscribed or held, which certificates or evidences of stock shall be transferable at the pleasure of the holder, in a suitable book or books to be kept by the company for that purpose, in person or by attorney duly authorized, in the presence of the president or treasurer, subject, however, to all payments due or to become due thereon; and the assignee or party to whom the same shall have been so transferred, shall be a member of said corporation, and have and enjoy all the immunities, privileges and franchises, and be subject to all the liabilities, conditions and penalties incident thereto, in the same manner as the original subscriber would have been. *Provided*, That no certificate shall be transferred so long as the holder thereof is indebted to said company, unless the board of directors shall consent thereto.

The capital stock may be called in, at the rate of $5 a share, every 60 days.

Public notice, for three successive weeks, to be given. (See sec. 4th.)

Stockholders liable to pay one per cent. a month on instalments due and unpaid.

If instalments and penalty, or a part, remain unpaid for six months, the shares may be forfeited.

Or suit may be brought.

Disposition of forfeited shares.

A stockholder cannot vote if a part or the

SECTION 9. The capital stock of the company shall be called in, and paid at such times and places, and in such proportions and instalments, not however exceeding five dollars per share, in any period of sixty days, as the directors shall require, of which public notice shall be given, for at least three successive weeks next preceding the time or times appointed for that purpose, in the newspapers last above mentioned; and if any stockholder shall neglect to pay such a proportion or instalment so called for, at the time and place appointed, he, she, or they, shall be liable to pay, in addition to the proportion or instalment so called for, at the rate of one per cent. per month for the delay of such payment; and if the same and the additional penalty, or any part thereof, shall remain unpaid for the period of six months, he, she or they shall, at the discretion of the directors, forfeit to the use of the company, all right, title and interest in, and to every and all share or shares, on account of which such default in payment may be made as aforesaid; or the directors may, at their option, cause suit to be brought before any competent tribunal, for the recovery of the amount due on such shares, together with the penalty of one per cent. per month as aforesaid; and in the event of a forfeiture, the share or shares so forfeited may be disposed of at the discretion of the president and directors, under such rules and regulations as may be prescribed by the by-laws; no stockholder shall be entitled to vote at any election, whole of any instalment be unpaid more than 30 days before election.

nor at any general or special meeting of the company, on whose share or shares any instalment or arrearages may be due, more than thirty days next preceding said election or meeting.

Dividends to be declared in May and November.

Payable after ten days from declaration Changed to 30 days by Sup. May 21, 1857, p. 40.

Dividends not to exceed the net profits of the company.

SECTION 10. That dividends of so much of the profits of said company, as shall appear advisable to the directors, shall be declared in the months of May and November, in each and every year, and be paid to the stockholders, or their legal representatives, on application at the office of said company, at any time after the expiration of ten days from the time of declaring the same; but the said dividends shall in no case exceed the amount of the net profits actually acquired by the company, so that the capital stock shall never be impaired thereby; and if the said directors shall make any dividend, which shall impair the capital stock of the company, the directors consenting thereto shall be liable, in their individual capacities, to the said company, for the amount of capital stock so divided, recoverable by action of debt, as in other cases; and each director present, when such dividend shall be declared, shall be considered as consenting thereto, unless he forthwith enter his protest on the minutes of the board, and give public notice to the stockholders of the declaring of such dividend. *Provided, however*, That after *bona fide* contracts shall have been made for the immediate construction of fifteen miles of road, at each end thereof, a sum equal to five per centum per annum, on all capital stock of said company actually paid in, shall be estimated and credited to the several holders thereof, on account of the amounts payable by them, respectively, for stock subscribed; and shall so continue to be estimated and credited, until one hundred miles of said railroad, that is to say: fifty miles thereof, commencing at the city of Pittsburgh and extending eastward, and fifty miles thereof, commencing at the easternmost terminus of said road, and extending westward, shall be completed and in use, which said estimates and credits shall be estimated and considered as part of the cost of construction: *And provided further*, That no dividends of profits shall be made, until one hundred miles of said railroad shall be completed, and in use, as is specified in the foregoing proviso; and if any loan of any part of the money received on the subscription to the stock be made to any officer, stockholder, or agent of the said company, or to any other person or corporation, it shall be deemed and taken as a violation and forfeiture of the charter authorized by this act, to be ascertained and declared, as provided in the twenty-fourth section of this act.

Directors consenting to make dividends out of the capital, to be liable therefor. (See 2d sec. Sup. 27th March, 1848, post, page 27.) Director to be considered as consenting unless he enters protest on the minutes forthwith.

When fifteen miles at each end of road are put under contract, 5 per cent. per annum to be credited on stock paid in. Provisoes repealed, 2d sec. Sup. 27th of March, 1848; see post, p. 27; but see last proviso to 2d sec. of this act, ante, p. 7.

When 50 miles road from each end are done and in use, the credit of 5 per cent. per annum to be discontinued.

No dividends to be made until 50 miles road at each end be done and in use.

A loan of any money received as stock to be taken as a violation and forfeiture of the charter.

SECTION 11. That the president and directors of said company, shall have power and authority by themselves, their engineers, superintendents, agents, artisans, and workmen, to survey, ascertain, locate, fix, mark and determine such route for a railroad as they may deem expedient, not however passing through any burying-ground, or place of public worship, or any dwelling-house, without the consent of the owner or owners thereof, and not, except in the neighborhood of deep cuttings or high embankments, or places selected for sidings, turn-outs, depots, engine or water stations, to exceed four rods in width, and thereon to lay down, erect, construct and establish a railroad with one or more tracks, with such branches or lateral roads as are hereinafter mentioned, and with such bridges, viaducts, turn-outs, sidings, or other devices, as they may deem necessary or useful, beginning at and uniting with the western terminus of the Harrisburg, Portsmouth, Mountjoy and Lancaster railroad, in the borough of Harrisburg. *Provided*, said Harrisburg, Portsmouth, Mountjoy and Lancaster Railroad Company shall be subject to, and consent to, the same rate of tax on tonnage for the use of the State, as is provided to be paid in this act by the Pennsylvania Railroad Company; and in case the said Harrisburg, Portsmouth, Mountjoy and Lancaster Railroad Company should not agree to comply with these conditions within three months after the distance of fifteen miles from Harrisburg westward shall *bona fide* be put under contract, the said Pennsylvania Railroad Company are authorized to connect their road with the Columbia Railroad, at or near the borough of Columbia, in Lancaster county: and thence by such direct practicable route, with moderate gradients, as will, in the opinion of the said president and directors, most conduce to the public interest and the interests of said company, having due regard to economy in the construction, maintenance and management thereof, and terminating at such point or points in, at, or near the city of Pittsburgh, or other place in the county of Allegheny, with authority to extend said road, or a branch thereof, to the town or harbour of Erie in the county of Erie, as to the said president and directors may seem most advantageous or expedient, and in like manner by themselves, or other persons by them appointed or employed as aforesaid, to enter into and upon, and occupy all land on which the said railroad or depots, warehouses, offices, toll-houses, engine and water stations, or other buildings or appurtenances hereinbefore mentioned, may be located, or which may be necessary or convenient for the erection of the same, or for any other purpose necessary or useful in the construction, maintenance or

Company to fix route, but not to pass through a grave yard, church or dwelling house. As to dwelling houses construed by 3d sect. Sup. 27th March, 1848, post, p. 27, and by 2d sec. Sup. 17th Feb. 1854, post, p. 36.

The ground to be taken for the railroad not to exceed 4 rods in width, except for deep cuts, sidings, depots, &c.

To unite with the Harrisburg railroad, if that company agree to the same tax on tonnage as this. See 6th sect. Act 27th of March, 1848, post, p. 25.

If the Harrisburg Company do not agree within 3 months after putting 15 miles under contract, then this company to connect with Columbia railroad.

The route to be direct, if practicable, with moderate gradients, to a point in, at, or near Pittsburgh.

A branch may be made to Erie.

The company may enter upon all lands necessary for such railroad.

repairs of said railroad, and therein and thereon to dig, excavate, and embank, make, grade, lay down and construct the same; and it shall in like manner be lawful for the said company, their officers, agents, engineers, contractors or workmen, with their implements and beasts of draft or burden, to enter upon any lands adjoining, or in the neighborhood of the said railroad so to be constructed, and to quarry, dig, cut, take and carry away therefrom any stone, gravel, clay, sand, earth, wood, or other suitable material necessary or proper for the construction, maintenance or repairing of said railroad, or for the construction of any bridges, viaducts, or other buildings which may be required for the use, maintenance, or repairs of said railroad: *Provided*, That such compensation shall be made, secured, or tendered to the owner or owners of any such lands or materials as shall be agreed upon between the parties, or in such manner as is hereafter mentioned: *Provided further*, That the timber used in the construction or repair of said railroad shall be obtained from the owners thereof only by agreement or purchase.

May cut and carry away material necessary for the making of the road.

Compensation to be made or tendered for the land and materials used.

Timber to be obtained only from the owners.

SECTION 12. That when the said company cannot agree with the owner or owners of any lands or materials, for the compensation proper for the damage done or likely to be done to, or sustained by, any such owner or owners of such lands or materials which said company may enter upon, use, or take away in pursuance of the authority hereinbefore given, or by reason of the absence or legal incapacity of any such owner or owners, no such compensation can be agreed upon, the Court of Quarter Sessions of the proper county, on application thereto by petition, either by said company or owner or owners, or any one in behalf of either, shall issue their precept to the sheriff of the county, commanding said sheriff to summon twenty discreet and disinterested persons, freeholders of said county, to act as jurors, and to meet at such convenient place near the premises, as in the said precept or by the said sheriff may be designated, in not less than ten, nor more than twenty days, giving such reasonable notice as the court may direct to both parties, by publication or otherwise, whose duty it shall be to ascertain and report to said court, whether any, and if any, what damages have been, or may be sustained by the owner or owners of said land or materials by reason of the construction of said railroad, or by reason of the materials used or taken away, in manner aforesaid; and if twelve or more of the said jurors attend, they shall be empanneled, and if twelve do not attend, the sheriff shall forthwith, or as soon thereafter as practicable, summon others to attend on a day by him fixed for that purpose; and the said twelve jurors being

This section repealed except as to proceedings commenced, by 4th sect. Sup. March 27, 1848. See post, p. 27. See also declaratory act, 5th April, 1849, post, p. 51.

Application to be made to the Court of Quarter Sessions of the proper county, for 20 freeholders to assess the damages done by the company.

Twelve jurors to be qualified and decide.

so empanneled, and having been first sworn or affirmed, by said sheriff, or his deputy, faithfully, justly and impartially to decide, and true report to make concerning all the matters and things to be submitted to them, and in relation to which they are authorized to inquire, in pursuance of the provisions of this act; and having viewed the premises, they shall estimate and determine the quantity, quality and value of said lands so taken or occupied, or to be so taken or occupied, or the materials so used or taken away, or to be so used or taken away, as the case may be, and having a due regard to, and making just allowance for the advantages which may have resulted, or which may seem likely to result to the owner or owners of said land or materials, in consequence of the opening or making of said railroad; and after having made a fair and just comparison of said advantages and disadvantages, they shall estimate and determine whether any, and if any, what amount of damages have been or may be sustained, and to whom payable, and make report thereof to the court; and if any damages be awarded, and the report be confirmed by said court, judgment shall be entered thereon, and if the amount thereof be not paid, execution may issue thereon, as in other cases of debt, for the sum so awarded; and the cost and expenses incurred shall be defrayed by said railroad company: *Provided*, That if said report be not confirmed, as aforesaid, and justice may seem to require it, a new inquisition may be ordered by said court: *And provided further*, That any owner or owners, or other party applying for a review, shall be liable for the costs of the proceedings prayed for, in case a report more favorable be not obtained upon such review: *And provided further, nevertheless*, That nothing herein contained shall authorize the said company to enter upon any lands, or take any property, without making compensation to the owners of said property, or giving adequate security therefor: *And be it further provided*, That in all cases where the parties cannot agree on the amount of damages claimed either for land or materials, the company shall tender a bond, with sufficient security, to the party claiming the damages; the condition of which shall be, that the company will pay, or cause to be paid, such amount of damages as the party shall be entitled to receive, after the same shall have been agreed upon by the parties, or assessed by the provisions of this act: *And provided further*, That in case the party or parties claiming damages refuse to accept the bond as tendered by the company, the company shall, in every such case, present their bonds to the Court of Common Pleas of the proper county; and if the court approve of the security, shall direct the same to be filed

The jury shall view the premises.

The jury to report the damages, and to whom payable.

The court may order a new inquisition.

Company not to enter upon land before paying or giving security therefor.

Where the company and parties cannot agree, the company shall give bond, with security, to pay the damages assessed.

If parties refuse to take the bond tendered, the company shall offer it for approval to the Court of Common Pleas of the county.

The bond if approved, shall be filed for the benefit of the parties entitled.

for the benefit of those to whom it is given, which bonds shall be answerable as all other debts for the amount of damages assessed, if the same be not paid in a reasonable time after such assessment.

The railroad must not impede the passage along any established road it may cross.

Wagon ways to be made for private persons whose lands the railroad divides.

SECTION 13. That whenever, in the construction of said road or roads, it shall be necessary to cross or intersect any established road or way, it shall be the duty of the president and directors of said company so to construct the said road across such established road or way, as not to impede the passage or transportation of persons or property along the same; or when it shall be necessary to pass through the land of any individual, it shall also be their duty to provide for such individual proper wagon ways across said road or roads, from one part of his lands to the other.

Service of process.

Action to be commenced within twelve months after the alleged cause occurred. General issue may be pleaded, and the special matter given in evidence.

SECTION 14. That in all suits or actions against the said company, the services of process on the president, secretary, treasurer, engineer, agent, or any director of said company, shall be good and available in law; but no suit or action shall be prosecuted by any person or persons, for any penalties incurred under this act, unless such suit or action shall be commenced within twelve months next after the offence committed, or cause of action accrued; and the defendants in such suit or action may plead the general issue, and give this act and the special matter in evidence, and that the same was done in pursuance and by authority of this act.

Injuries to the railroad to be punished by threefold the damages sustained.

SECTION 15. That if any person or persons shall wilfully and knowingly break, injure, or destroy the railroad hereby authorized, or any part thereof, or any edifice, device, property or work, or any part thereof, or any machinery, engine, car, implement or utensil, erected, owned or used by the said company, in pursuance of this act, he, she, or they so offending, shall forfeit and pay to the said company three times the actual damage so sustained, to be sued for and recovered, with full costs, before any tribunal having cognizance thereof, by action in the name and for the use of said company.

Persons wilfully obstructing the railroad punishable in the penitentiary.

Civil remedy also may be pursued.

SECTION 16. That if any person or persons shall wilfully and maliciously remove or destroy any of the company's constructions, or place designedly and with evil intent, any obstruction on the line of said railroad, so as to jeopard the safety, or endanger the lives of persons traveling on or over the same, such person or persons so offending shall be deemed guilty of a misdemeanor, and shall, on conviction, be imprisoned in the penitentiary for a term not less than three months, nor more than three years: *Provided*, That nothing herein contained shall prevent the company from pursuing any other appropriate remedy at law in such cases.

Owners of land may make lateral railroads for conveying the products of the same land.

SECTION 17. That the said company shall not prevent any person or persons, being the owner or owners of land bordering on or adjacent to said railroad, from making lateral railroads, and connecting the same with the railroad of the company, for the purpose of transporting thereon their produce or other material, being the products of said land; the said connections being made at the expense of the person or persons wishing the same, and according to the directions and subject to the approval of the directors of said company, or their authorized agent; and it shall be lawful for the said company, in the manner, and subject to the conditions and provisions hereinbefore provided in relation to the main line of their railroad by this act authorized to be made, to make such lateral railroads or branches, leading from the main line of their said railroad, to such convenient place or points, in either of the counties into or through which the said main line of their road may pass, as the president and directors may deem advantageous, and suited to promote the convenience of the inhabitants thereof, and the interests of said company.

The company may construct branches from main line in any county.

Troops and munitions of war to be carried at half price.

SECTION 18. That in times of war, invasion, or domestic insurrection, the said company shall carry and transport, or permit to be carried and transported on said railroad, any troops called into service by any competent authority, their ordnance, munitions and military stores, at one-half the usual charge for the time being for carrying and transporting other passengers and freight.

A full report to be annually made by the President and Directors to the stockholders. October changed to December. See 3d section, Sup. of 26th of April, 1850, post, p. 32.

SECTION 19. That at each annual meeting of the stockholders of said company, the president and directors, for the year preceding, shall lay before them a full and complete statement of the affairs of the company for the year ending on the last day of October immediately preceding, exhibiting, under the various appropriate heads, the amount of moneys received, and from what sources, the amount disbursed, and for what purpose, the balance remaining with the company; which statement shall be accompanied with a report of the acts and proceedings of the company for the same period, with such further information as may be requisite to convey to the stockholders a full knowledge of the affairs and condition of said company; the said statement and report shall be published, as soon as conveniently may be, in pamphlet form, and in such newspapers as the stockholders or president and directors may designate, and a copy thereof shall be transmitted to the Governor, and to each branch of the Legislature, at its next annual meeting.

Annual report to be published in pamphlet form and in newspapers.

The stockholders may increase the capital

SECTION 20. That if any increase of the capital stock shall be deemed necessary, in order to complete or improve the said railroad stock to ten millions. Increased. See post, pp. 33, 34, 38, 48, 62.

or appurtenances, it shall be lawful for the stockholders of said company, at any annual meeting, or at any special meeting convened for that purpose, in manner as aforesaid, to increase and dispose of any additional number of shares, not exceeding fifty thousand, so that the whole amount of said capital stock shall not exceed ten millions of dollars, and receive and demand the moneys for the said additional shares, in like manner and subject to the same conditions hereinbefore provided for the original subscriptions, or as shall be provided for in the by-laws of said company.

The railroad, and each part as finished, to be a public highway.

SECTION 21. That upon the completion of said railroad, or any part thereof, the same shall be esteemed a public highway, for the conveyance of passengers and the transportation of freight, subject to such rules and regulations in relation to the same, and to the size and construction of wheels, cars and carriages, the weight of loads, and all other matters and things connected with the use of said railroad, as the president and directors may prescribe and direct: *Provided*, That the said company shall have the exclusive control of the motive power, and may from time to time establish, demand, and receive, such rates of toll or other compensation, for the use of the said road, and of said motive power, and for the conveyance of passengers, the transportation of merchandise and commodities, and the cars or other vehicles containing the same, or otherwise passing over or on said railroad, as to the president and directors shall seem reasonable: *Provided, however, nevertheless*, That said rates of toll and motive power charges, so to be established, demanded or received, when the cars used for such conveyance or transportation are owned or furnished by others, shall not exceed two and a half cents per mile for each passenger; three cents per mile for each ton of two thousand pounds for freight; three cents per mile for each passenger or baggage car, and two cents per mile for each burden or freight car, every four wheels being computed a car; and in the transportation of passengers, no charge shall be made to exceed three cents per mile for through passengers, and three and a half cents per mile for way passengers.

The company to have control of the motive power, and establish rates of toll.

Rates of toll and motive power, 2½ cents a mile for a passenger, and 3 cents a ton for freight, where cars are not owned by the company.

Rates of toll and motive power.

Tonnage regulated between 10th March and 1st December. Commuted, see 4th proviso to the 1st sect. of the Supplement passed 27th March, 1848, post, p. 26.

SECTION 22. That all tonnage, of whatsoever kind or description, except the ordinary baggage of passengers, loaded or received at Harrisburg or Pittsburgh, or at any intermediate point, and carried or conveyed on or over said railroad, more than twenty miles, between the tenth day of March and the first day of December in each and every year, shall be subject to a toll or duty, for the use of the commonwealth, at the rate of five mills per mile for each ton of two thousand pounds; and it shall be the duty of said company, between the twentieth and thirtieth days of July, and between the first and tenth days of December, in each and every year, after thirty miles or more of said railroad shall have been completed and in use, to cause to be made out, and filed with the auditor general, a true and correct statement, exhibiting the amount of such tonnage so loaded or received, and the distance so carried or conveyed, during the respective periods intervening between the said tenth day of March and the twentieth day of July, and between the said twentieth day of July and the first day of December, in each and every year; which said statement shall be verified by the oath or affirmation of the receiving or forwarding agent or agents, or other proper officer or officers of said company having knowledge of the premises; and at the time of filing said statement, or on or before the said thirtieth day of July and the tenth day of December, in each and every year, the said company shall pay to the State Treasurer the amount of said toll or duty so accruing for the use of the Commonwealth, during the respective intervening periods before mentioned. *Provided*, That if it shall hereafter be deemed necessary or expedient, the Governor may appoint one or more State agents, not exceeding three, who shall have the right at all times to travel free of charge on or over said railroad, between Harrisburg and Pittsburgh, in the cars or other vehicles of the company used for the conveyance of passengers; and at all times, during the usual hours of business, shall have free access to, and liberty to inspect and examine all such books, accounts, way-bills, bills of freight, manifests and other papers of the company, as may be necessary and proper to enable the said agent or agents to ascertain and keep a true and correct account of all such tonnage so loaded, received, carried or transported on or over said railroad, during the periods aforesaid; and the Legislature hereby reserves the right to adopt such additional measures to secure a faithful compliance with the conditions of this proviso, as may hereafter be deemed right and proper.

Report of tonnage to be made to the Auditor General after 30 miles of railroad shall have been completed.

Payment of the sum due, to be made to the State Treasurer.

The Governor may appoint State agents, if necessary, to keep an account of tonnage transported.

State agents may examine all books of the company for this purpose.

SECTION 23. That if the Legislature of this State shall, at the expiration of twenty years from the completion of said railroad, make provision by law for the repayment to the said company of the amount expended by them in the construction of said railroad, and in the construction of permanent fixtures, and all other appurtenances for the use of the same, together with all moneys expended by said company, for repairs, attendance and otherwise, for the purpose of said railroad, with interest on such sums at the rate of eight per cent. per annum, after deducting the amount of tolls and other revenue received by said company for the use of the same,

The State may purchase the railroad at the end of 20 years.

Repealed. Act of May 16, 1857, sec. 3, p. 64.

The terms of purchase.

then said railroad, with all its fixtures and appurtenances, shall vest in and become the property of the people of this State; but if the Legislature shall not, at the expiration of the said period of twenty years, claim the said railroad, and so forth, as aforesaid, then the said company, with all its said rights and privileges, shall continue for another period of twenty years, subject to the claim of the Legislature, as aforesaid, at the expiration thereof, on the same terms and conditions as aforesaid, and so on from twenty years to twenty years.

The company to enjoy their rights for 20 years more, if not bought by the State.

The books, &c., of the company to be open to a committee of the Legislature.

SECTION 24. That it shall at all times be lawful for a committee of the Legislature, appointed for that purpose, to inspect the books and examine into the proceedings of the corporation hereby created, and to report whether the provisions of this charter have been by the same abused or violated; and if the officers of said corporation shall refuse to be sworn or affirmed, or give evidence, or refuse to produce any of their books or papers that may be demanded, before any such committee, then the Legislature may, by law, declare the said charter void, and repeal the same; and whenever any committee as aforesaid shall find and report, or the Governor shall have reason to believe that the charter has been violated, it may be lawful for the Legislature to direct, or the Governor to order, a *scire facias* to be sued out of the Supreme Court of Pennsylvania, in the name of the Commonwealth of Pennsylvania, which shall be served by the sheriff of any county in this Commonwealth on the president, treasurer or secretary, at the office of the corporation, for the time being, at least ten days before the commencement of the term of court, calling on the said corporation to show cause why the charter hereby granted should not be declared forfeited; and it shall be lawful for the said court, upon the return of the *scire facias*, to examine into the truth of the alleged violations; and if such violations be made to appear, then to adjudge that the said charter is forfeited, and thereupon, and in case the Legislature shall have power to declare the said charter void, and to repeal the same for the cause aforesaid, the railroad aforesaid, with its appurtenances, and all estate, real and personal, of the said corporation, shall revert to and be vested in the Commonwealth, upon the payment by the Commonwealth, to the stockholders, the par value of their stock; and until the Commonwealth shall have made such payment to the president and directors of said company, to be by them distributed among the stockholders, the rights, privileges and franchises of said corporation shall remain as though said judgment and forfeiture had not been pronounced or declared: *Provided, however,* That

Refusal to produce, &c., may be a cause of forfeiture.

Proceedings to ascertain a cause of forfeiture.

The Commonwealth to pay stockholders the par value of stock in case of forfeiture.

Issue of fact to be tried by a jury.

every issue of fact, which may be joined between the Commonwealth and the corporation, in said proceedings, shall be tried by a jury, summoned by an officer to be named by the court, from the body of the State, and it shall be lawful for the court aforesaid to require and compel the production of such of the books and papers of the corporation on such trial, as it may deem necessary for the ascertainment of the controverted facts; and the final judgment of the court shall be subject to all the usages of law as in other cases. The first twenty of the commissioners appointed in the first section of this act, or any five of them, shall have authority to convene the commissioners at such suitable time and place as they may designate for that purpose, giving sufficient notice thereof, as the occasion may seem to require. And all reasonable expenses incurred by the commissioners in the performance of the duties by this act imposed, shall be allowed and paid by the corporation out of the first instalment or payment, to be received by the commissioners at the time of subscribing, as hereinbefore provided.

Corporation to pay the expenses incurred by Commissioners, out of first instalment.

Railroad to be commenced in two and completed within ten years, and not to remain impassable for two years. See Sup. 13th April, 1846, post, p. 25. Charter extended for 10 years. Act April 16, 1857, post, p. 9.

SECTION 25. That if the said company shall not commence the construction of said railroad within two years, and complete and open the same for use, with one or more tracks, within the term of ten years; or if, after the completion, the said railroad shall be suffered to go into decay, and be impassable for the term of two years, then this charter shall be null and void, except so far as relates to the payment of damages.

SECTION 26. That if any person or persons traveling on the road of the said company, or that of any other company in this Commonwealth, shall be wounded by reason of any imperfection or defect in such road, or in the machinery or cars employed on the same, or by the negligence of such company or their agents, no action brought by such person or persons against such company, to recover damages therefor, shall abate by the death of the plaintiff or plaintiffs, but the same shall survive to his or her executors or administrators.

Action against company not to abate by death of plaintiff.

SECTION 27. The Legislature reserves the right to authorize any company hereafter chartered to connect any railroad not running parallel with the same, to be constructed by such company, with the railroad of the said Pennsylvania Railroad Company, at such point or points on said railroad as the Legislature may direct. *Provided*, That no higher rates of toll or of transportation shall be charged by said company, for persons or things having passed, or destined to pass, over such connecting road, than may be at the same time charged upon persons and things passing over the main line to and from Philadelphia and Pittsburgh.

Right reserved to charter another railroad to connect, but *not to run parallel with this.*

Approved April 13th, 1846.

SUPPLEMENTS TO CHARTER.

AN ACT

SUPPLEMENTARY TO AN ACT TO INCORPORATE THE PENNSYLVANIA RAILROAD COMPANY, PASSED APRIL, EIGHTEEN HUNDRED AND FORTY-SIX.

Construction of act to which this is a supplement.

SECTION 1. That nothing in the act to which this is a supplement shall be so construed as in anywise to impair the right of the Legislature to pass such additional laws as may be deemed expedient in furtherance of the objects contemplated by said act, and for the better enforcement of the provisions thereof; and, in case the charter of said company shall be forfeited in the manner therein provided, it shall be competent for the Legislature by law to vest the said railroad and appurtenances, and all the estate, real and personal, of the said company, in the Commonwealth, or in another company to be incorporated for that purpose, upon the payment to said Pennsylvania Railroad Company, for distribution amongst the stockholders, according to their several interests, the actual value of their said railroad appurtenances and other property, to be ascertained and appraised by twelve disinterested persons, acting under oath or affirmation, to be appointed and governed in their proceedings in relation thereto, in such manner as the Legislature shall by law direct. *Provided*, That in case the said company shall at any time fail to pay the toll or charge on tonnage, which may accrue or become due to the Commonwealth under the provisions of said act, the same shall be and remain a lien on the property of the said company, and shall have precedence over all other liens or incumbrances thereon, until paid.

In case of forfeiture, the State to pay the actual value of corporate estate to company.

Charge on tonnage a lien.

Approved April 13th, 1846.

A FURTHER SUPPLEMENT

TO AN ACT TO INCORPORATE THE PENNSYLVANIA RAILROAD COMPANY, PASSED APRIL THIRTEENTH, ONE THOUSAND EIGHT HUNDRED AND FORTY-SIX.

Allegheny county, cities of Pittsburgh and Allegheny, and municipal corporations of Philadelphia county and Philadelphia city, made competent to subscribe for stock.

SECTION 1. That under the provisions of the first section of the act, entitled "An Act to incorporate the Pennsylvania Railroad Company," approved the thirteenth day of April, one thousand eight hundred and forty-six, it shall be competent to the county of Allegheny, the cities of Pittsburgh and Allegheny, and the municipal corporations in the county of Philadelphia, and the said act shall be construed to have authorized the city of Philadelphia to subscribe for shares in the capital stock of said Pennsylvania Railroad Company, and to borrow money to pay therefor, and to make provision for the payment of the principal and interest of the money so borrowed, as in other cases of loans to said corporations; and no certificate or bond issued shall be for a less sum than one hundred dollars, and shall be transferable only on the books of the respective corporations kept for that purpose; and the certificates of loan or bonds issued, or to be issued, by any such corporations for the purpose aforesaid, bearing an interest of six per centum per annum, payable half-yearly, may be received as cash by the company named in said act, in payment of the instalments on shares subscribed by such corporation; but the total amount of the shares in the capital stock aforesaid, subscribed for by any such corporation, shall not exceed five per cent. on the assessed value of the property subject to taxation for state or county purposes, within the limits of such corporation: *Provided*, That any city or other municipal corporation, or the county of Allegheny aforesaid, may be represented at elections and at other meetings of the said company, by agents duly authorized by the commissioners of said counties, and by the mayor or chief officers of said cities, or other municipal corporations, acting under resolutions passed by the constituted authorities thereof: *Provided also*, That any county, city, or municipal corporation, that shall be possessed of ten thousand or more shares in the capital stock of said company, shall, in lieu of voting at the general elections of said company hereafter, be entitled by the constituted authorities thereof, to elect one director out of the number designated in the act to which this is a supplement, within one month prior to the first Monday in December, for each and every ten thousand shares held by said corporation; but no county or corporation shall be entitled to elect more than three directors, and a majority of the board of directors shall, at all times, be elected by the private stockholders; if at any time the corporations who have subscribed to the stock shall be entitled, under this provision, to more than six directors, then the number of directors to which such corporation (as elect more than one director) is entitled to, shall be reduced in such manner as shall be determined upon by the directors in office, so as to do justice to all: *Provided further*, That all directors elected by said corporations shall be possessed of not less than twenty shares of the stock of said company, in their own right, and shall not be members of the body by which they are elected: *Provided further*, That the tax on tonnage of five mills per ton per mile, from the

Authorized to borrow money.

Amount of such subscription.

Proviso.

Proviso.

When corporations may elect directors. Never entitled to more than three.

Private stockholders always to elect majority of the board.

Proviso.

Proviso. Tax on tonnage. See 22d sec. Act 13th April, 1846. Ante, p. 18.

tenth of March to the first of December, payable to the State treasury under the provisions of the twenty-second section of the act to which this is a supplement, be commuted to a tax of three mills per ton per mile during the whole year; and if, after two years from the completion of the road, the commutation to three mills herein provided shall not yield as much revenue to the Commonwealth as would have been received under the original provision, then the rate of five mills, as originally provided for, may be restored at the option of the Legislature; said tax to cover all freight carried over the road more than twenty miles.

Coal and Lumber exempted. See Act of May 7, 1855, p. 56.

SECTION 2. That the directors of the Pennsylvania Railroad Company be and are hereby authorized to pay to the shareholders entitled to receive the same, in the months of May and November, in each year, interest at the rate of six per cent. per annum, on all instalments paid by them, which interest shall be charged to the cost of construction, and continue to pay the same until the said road shall be completed; and that, until the period for which a dividend shall be declared, all the profits and earnings of the said railroad shall be credited to the cost of construction: *Provided*, That no stockholder who has neglected, or who hereafter shall neglect to pay up the instalments as called for, shall be entitled to receive interest on the same; and the directors of said railroad company are hereby required strictly to enforce the penalty which is provided in the case of delinquencies under the act to which this is a supplement; and the provisoes to the tenth section be and the same are hereby repealed: *Provided further*, That the stock of said company shall not be subject to any tax in consequence of the payment of the interest hereby authorized.

Railroad company to pay interest semi-annually.

Proviso.

Stockholder neglecting to pay his instalments not to receive interest.

Provisoes to 10th sec. Act 13th April, 1846, repealed. See last proviso to 2d sec. of the original act.

Proviso. Ante, p. 7.

SECTION 3. That so much of the eleventh section of said act, as prohibits the Pennsylvania Railroad Company from passing through any dwelling-house, shall be construed only to extend to homesteads in possession and occupancy of the owner or owners, and shall not extend to dwellings kept for rent: *Provided*, That full compensation be made to the owner or owners of such buildings, for all damage sustained thereby, the same to be ascertained as in other cases.

Construction of 11th sec. of act of incorporation. Ante, p. 18.

Proviso.

SECTION 4. That when the Pennsylvania Railroad Company cannot agree with the owner or owners of any lands or materials, for the compensation proper for the damage done, or likely to be done to, or sustained by any such owner or owners of such lands or materials which said company may enter upon, use, or take away in pursuance of the authority given them by the act to which this is a

Damages, how to be assessed.

supplement, or by reason of the absence or legal incapacity of any such owner or owners, no such compensation can be agreed upon, the court of common pleas of the proper county, on application thereto, by petition, either by said company or owner or owners, or any one in behalf of either, shall appoint five disinterested persons of the next adjoining county or counties, none of whom shall be residents of any of the counties through which said railroad shall pass, and to fix a time, not less than twenty, nor more than thirty days thereafter, for said viewers to meet upon the premises where the damages are alleged to be sustained, of which time and place ten days' notice shall be given by the party petitioning to said viewers, and to the other party, and the said viewers having been first sworn or affirmed by some power competent to administer oaths, faithfully, justly and impartially to decide, and true report to make concerning all the matters and things to be submitted to them, and in relation to which they are authorized to inquire, in pursuance of the provisions of this act; and having viewed the premises, they shall estimate and determine the quantity, quality and value of said lands so taken or occupied, or to be taken and occupied, or the materials so used or taken away, or to be used or taken away, as the case may be, and having a due regard to, and making just allowances for the advantages which may have resulted, or which may seem likely to result to the owner or owners of said lands or materials, in consequence of the opening or making of said railroad, or the construction of works connected therewith; and after having made a fair and just comparison of said advantages or disadvantages, they shall estimate and determine whether any, and if any, what amount of damages have been sustained or may be sustained, and to whom payable, and make report thereof to the court; and if any damages be awarded, and the report be confirmed by said court, judgment shall be entered thereon, and if the amount thereof be not paid, execution may issue thereon as in other cases of debt, for the sum so awarded; and the cost and expenses incurred shall be defrayed by said railroad company; and the said viewers shall be entitled to two dollars per day for each of them, for the time necessarily employed in performing the duties hereinbefore prescribed: *Provided*, That nothing herein contained shall authorize the said company to enter upon any lands, or take any property without making compensation to the owners of said property, or give adequate security therefor: *And provided*, That if either, or all of the judges of the court of common pleas aforesaid, is or are interested in the said railroad as officers, stockholders, contractors, or otherwise, then the

Court of common pleas of proper county to appoint viewers.

See 1st sec. of an act entitled "A further Supplement," &c., approved 26th April, 1850, post, p. 32.

Judgment and execution for the damages.

Compensation of viewers. See post, p. 37.

Proviso.

Proviso. When judges are interested.

viewers aforesaid shall be selected and appointed by the sheriff and commissioners of the proper county, in like manner and with like powers, as if appointed by the court of common pleas: *Provided further*, That if the proper officer of said company, at any time before application made by either party for the appointment of viewers, in the manner hereinbefore directed, shall tender to the owner or owners of said lands or materials a sum of money, in full compensation for his or their said damages, said company shall not be liable for costs on any subsequent proceedings, unless such owner or owners of land or materials shall be awarded a larger sum than the previous tender of said company: *Provided*, That in all cases where proceedings have been instituted under the twelfth section of the act of the thirteenth April, one thousand eight hundred and forty-six, the same shall be continued and proceeded in according to the provisions of the aforesaid act.

When tender of damages will relieve from costs.

Proviso. See declaratory Act 5th April, 1849, post. p. 31.

SECTION 5. That if said railroad company shall find it necessary to change the site of any portion of any turnpike or public road, they shall cause the same to be reconstructed forthwith, at their own proper expense, on the most favorable location, and in as perfect a manner as the original road: *Provided*, That the damages incurred in changing the location of any road authorized by this section, shall be ascertained and paid by said company, in the same manner as is provided for in regard to the location and construction of their own road.

Crossing or occupying turnpike roads, to reconstruct the same.

See sec. 1, Act of April 12, 1851, p. 45, and Sup. 20th March, 1849, post, p. 30.

SECTION 6. That the first proviso contained in the eleventh section of the act to which this is a supplement, shall be so construed as to extend exclusively to such tonnage as shall have, under the twenty-second section of said act, become liable to taxation on its transit over the Pennsylvania Railroad, and that said road, referred to in said proviso, shall terminate at or near the city of Pittsburgh.

Construction of first proviso of 11th sec. of act of incorporation

SECTION 7. That the said Pennsylvania Railroad Company be and are hereby authorized to connect their railroad with the Allegheny Portage Railroad, by the most practicable route, at such points at or near Hollidaysburg and Johnstown, as may be agreed upon with the canal commissioners.

To connect with Allegheny Portage Railroad.

Approved March 27th, 1848.

A SUPPLEMENT

TO THE ACT INCORPORATING THE PENNSYLVANIA RAILROAD COMPANY.

Preamble.

WHEREAS, The Legislature, by the fifth section of an act passed the twenty-seventh March, one thousand eight hundred and forty-eight, entitled "A further supplement to An Act to incorporate the Pennsylvania Railroad Company," did provide, That if said railroad company shall find it necessary to change the site of any portion of any turnpike or public road, they shall cause the same to be reconstructed forthwith, at their own proper expense, in the most favorable location, and in as perfect a manner as the original road; but there is no provision made for compelling the said company to comply with this law; therefore,

When the site of any portion of a turnpike or public road is changed, and not reconstructed within the proper time, application to be made to the Court of Quarter Sessions.

SECTION 1. *Be it enacted, &c.*, That if in the construction of their road by the Pennsylvania Railroad Company, it shall have been or may hereafter be necessary to change the site of any portion of any turnpike or public road, when the necessary time shall have elapsed to have enabled the said railroad company to comply with the provisions of the fifth section of the act of the twenty-seventh March, one thousand eight hundred and forty-eight, requiring them to re-construct such turnpike or public road, it shall be the duty of the Court of Quarter Sessions of the county in which such turnpike or public road shall be located, upon the petition of the company owning the said turnpike, or of any twelve or more citizens of the township in which the said public road may be, to appoint three competent persons, citizens from an adjoining county, through which the said road does not pass, as viewers, whose duty it shall be to view the place where the said turnpike or public road was, and make report to the said court at their next session, whether the said Pennsylvania Railroad Company have complied with their duty in making said turnpike or public road as they are required by the said law to do; and if the said viewers shall report to the said court that the Pennsylvania Railroad Company has complied with the provisions of the said act of Assembly, and the said report shall be approved by the court, an order shall be then made, that the costs and expenses of the said view shall be paid by the petitioners; but if the said viewers shall report to the said court, that the said company has not complied with the provisions of the said act of Assembly, and the said report shall be approved by the court, the expenses

Who to make the application.

Viewers to be appointed, and their duties.

Order of court when viewers report that the railroad company has complied with act of Assembly.

Who to pay costs.

Order when report is against the company.

thereof shall be paid by the said railroad company; then it shall be the duty of the said court to order and decree that the said turnpike or public road, as the case may be, shall be made, finished and completed as the said Pennsylvania Railroad Company, by the provisions of the said fifth section of the act of twenty seventh March, one thousand eight hundred and forty-eight, were bound to finish and complete the same: *Provided*, That if either party shall be dissatisfied with the decree, they may have the right to a review under the provisions of this act. Right to a review.

Approved March 20th, 1849.

AN ACT

DECLARATORY OF THE FOURTH SECTION OF AN ACT SUPPLEMENTARY TO THE CHARTER OF THE PENNSYLVANIA RAILROAD COMPANY, APPROVED MARCH TWENTY-SEVENTH, ONE THOUSAND EIGHT HUNDRED AND FORTY-EIGHT.

SECTION 1. That the last proviso to the fourth section of the supplement to the act to incorporate the Pennsylvania Railroad Company, passed the twenty seventh day of March, one thousand eight hundred and forty-eight, shall be so construed, that those cases wherein proceedings have been commenced under the twelfth section of the act of the thirteenth of April, one thousand eight hundred and forty-six, and have been proceeded in, shall be continued to final judgment and execution under and according to the provisions of the act of one thousand eight hundred and forty-six, which, as well as the said proviso, shall remain in full force for that purpose. Construction of the last proviso to the 4th sect. of supplement of 27th March, 1848. Ante, p. 29.

Approved April 5th, 1849.

A FURTHER SUPPLEMENT

TO THE ACT INCORPORATING THE PENNSYLVANIA RAILROAD COMPANY.

Compensation of viewers and their powers. See ante, sec. 4, p. 28.

SECTION 1. That the viewers appointed for the purpose of assessing damages in pursuance of the act of the twenty-seventh of March, Anno Domini one thousand eight hundred and forty-eight, entitled "An Act to incorporate the Pennsylvania Railroad Company," be entitled to receive as a compensation two dollars per day while engaged in said business; that one or more of said viewers shall have power to adjourn from day to day, and that a majority of the said viewers so appointed shall have power to view and assess damages, and to report as fully and with like effect as though all were present. *And provided further*, That a penalty of ten dollars be imposed on any of the said viewers who shall neglect or refuse to attend after appointment and due notice, at the time and place named, unless unavoidably prevented; said penalty to be recoverable before any justice of the peace, as debts of similar amount are recoverable, for the use of the person suing for the same.

Penalty of ten dollars for neglect of duty.

Stockholders to meet on the 1st Monday of February annually. See ante, p. 8.

SECTION 2. That hereafter the stockholders of the said Pennsylvania Railroad Company shall meet on the first Monday of February, in every year; and that so much of the fourth section of the act, entitled "An Act to incorporate the Pennsylvania Railroad Company," approved the thirteenth day of April, one thousand eight hundred and forty six, as prescribes the first Monday in December as the day of the annual meeting, is hereby repealed.

At the annual meetings, president and directors to report to the stockholders up to the last of December immediately preceding. See sec. 19th, act of incorporation, ante, p. 17.

SECTION 3. That at each annual meeting of the stockholders of said company, the president and directors for the year preceding shall lay before them a full and complete statement of the affairs of the company for the year ending on the last day of December immediately preceding, and that so much of the nineteenth section of the act aforesaid, as prescribes the last day of October as the day to which such statement shall be completed, is hereby repealed.

Approved April 26th, 1850.

A FURTHER SUPPLEMENT

TO THE ACT ENTITLED "AN ACT TO INCORPORATE THE PENNSYLVANIA RAILROAD COMPANY."

SECTION 1. That to enable the Pennsylvania Railroad Company to complete, stock, and equip their railroad with its appurtenances, and from time to time to lay down a double track therefor by means of subscription to the capital stock, it shall be lawful for the said company, in addition to the said capital stock authorized by the twentieth section of the act incorporating said company, passed on the thirteenth day of April, eighteen hundred and forty-six, to issue certificates for any additional sum not exceeding sixty thousand shares, and to demand and receive moneys for the same for said additional shares when subscribed for, in like manner, and upon the same conditions as to instalments and otherwise, as are provided for in the ninth section of said original act: *Provided*, That the par value of said additional capital stock shall be fifty dollars per share, as heretofore, and that the holders thereof shall have all the rights and immunities which are by law vested in the subscribers to the capital stock originally authorized to be created.

Pennsylvania Railroad Co. to issue additional certificates of stock. See ante, p. 17.

Proviso.

SECTION 2. That the said Pennsylvania Railroad Company are hereby authorized to purchase and hold the title to two several estates situated in West Philadelphia, and county of Philadelphia, owned now, or late, by the city of Philadelphia, and the Board of Health, respectively, and also to purchase and hold the title to any portion of the Powelton estate, for the purpose of erecting thereon offices, station houses, warehouses, shops, car sheds, sidings, cattle yards, and for such other objects as appertain to the legitimate business of the company, authorized by their act of incorporation, of transporting passengers and tonnage over their road and the Columbia Railroad, not exceeding thirty acres of uplands; the boundaries of such quantity of land as said company may deem proper to take, to be determined by the President of the company, and the Governor of the State of Pennsylvania, or the President of the Board of Canal Commissioners; also the right to purchase and hold within the city of Philadelphia, such other property for depots, offices, and sidings, as may be necessary or convenient for the transaction of the proper business of said company, authorized by their act of incorporation.

To hold certain real estate.

SECTION 3. That Eighth street and Plumb alley, in the city of Pittsburgh, and all other streets that extend through the property of

Certain streets in city of Pittsburgh vacated.

the Pennsylvania Railroad Company, are hereby vacated, and the title thereof vested in the said company: *Provided*, That the councils of said city give their assent thereto, and the same shall be filed in the Court of Quarter Sessions of Allegheny county.

Proviso.

Lease of levee on Monongahela river confirmed.

SECTION 4. That the right of the Councils of the city of Pittsburgh, to lease to the said railroad company the levee on the Monongahela river, below Liberty street, is hereby recognized and confirmed.

Approved April 23d, 1852.

A FURTHER SUPPLEMENT

TO THE ACT ENTITLED "AN ACT TO INCORPORATE THE PENNSYLVANIA RAILROAD COMPANY."

Pennsylvania railroad Co. authorized to subscribe stock in certain cases.

SECTION 1. That the Pennsylvania Railroad Company be and they are hereby authorized and empowered to subscribe to the capital stock, or guarantee the bonds of such railroad companies in other States, as may seem to them important to promote the trade of Pennsylvania and the interest of the company, such subscription not to exceed fifteen per cent. of the capital stock actually subscribed to the said Pennsylvania Railroad Company, and to pay for the same in such manner as the directors of said Pennsylvania Railroad Company may determine: *Provided*, That said company shall give thirty days' notice, which notice shall be during the session of the Supreme Court, in at least one newspaper published in the City of Philadelphia, and one newspaper published in the City of Pittsburgh, of any intended subscription or guarantee under the provisions of this act, and it shall be the duty of the Supreme Court to proceed without delay, within the said thirty days, to hear and determine any application for a preliminary injunction, by any stockholder in said company, to restrain said company from making such subscription or guarantee.

Proviso.

Pennsylvania Railroad Co. to issue additional certificates of stock. See ante, pp. 17, 33.

SECTION 2. That for the purpose of meeting the subscriptions authorized by the foregoing section, and to enable them to construct their double track, it shall be lawful for the said Pennsylvania Railroad Company, in addition to thesaid capital stock authorized by the twentieth section of the act incorporating said company, passed on the thirteenth day of April, one thousand eight hundred and forty-six, and the several supplements thereto, to issue certificates for any additional sums, not exceeding eighty thousand shares, and to demand and receive moneys for the same when subscribed for, in like manner, and also on the same conditions as to instalments and otherwise, as are provided for in the ninth section of said original act of incorporation: *Provided*, That the said additional capital stock shall be fifty dollars per share, as heretofore, and that the holders thereof shall have all the rights and immunities which are by law invested in the subscribers to the capital stock originally authorized to be created: *And provided further*, That no such certificate hereby authorized to be issued, shall be for a less sum than one hundred dollars.

Proviso.

Proviso.

Section 3. That the directors of the Pennsylvania Railroad Company be and they are hereby authorized to add to their number, by electing from the body of the stockholders, at such time as they may determine, and annually thereafter, if they deem it expedient, one person, who shall act as vice-president of said company, with such powers and for such compensation as the said board shall by by-law or resolution establish and direct.

Authority to elect vice president.

Approved March 23d, 1853.

A FURTHER SUPPLEMENT

TO AN ACT TO INCORPORATE THE PENNSYLVANIA RAILROAD COMPANY, PASSED APRIL THIRTEENTH, ONE THOUSAND EIGHT HUNDRED AND FORTY-SIX.

Section 1. That in proceedings by the Pennsylvania Railroad Company, for the appropriation of land under any Act of Assembly, when it shall appear to the Court of Common Pleas, by affidavit or otherwise, that there is a disputed, doubtful or defective title, or that any party in interest is absent, covert, not of full age, or from any cause incapable of being served with notice, or of having a bond tendered within the county where the land is situated, the said court shall, on application of the said company, direct the filing of a bond in an amount, and with security, to the commonwealth, to be approved by the court, for the use of the party found to be entitled thereto, and shall direct notice thereof, and of the petition to assess damages, and the meeting of viewers, to be published in two news-

How notice to be served and bond tendered in proceedings to appropriate land, where title is doubtful, &c., or party interested absent, covert, under age, or otherwise incapable of being served.

papers of the county where the land is situated, for two weeks before the day appointed for the meeting of the viewers; and the said bond so filed, and the said notice so given, shall have like effect as if the provisions of the twelfth section of the Act of Assembly, entitled "An Act to incorporate the Pennsylvania Railroad Company," approved April thirteenth, one thousand eight hundred and forty-six, in regard to giving bond, had been fully complied with, and as if personal notice had been served on the party owning the said lands, as provided for by the fourth section of an act entitled "A further supplement to an act to incorporate the Pennsylvania Railroad Company," passed April thirteenth one thousand eight hundred and forty-six, approved the twenty-seventh day of March, one thousand eight hundred and forty-eight.

Effect of such notice and bond.

11th sec. of act of April 13, 1846, shall not be construed to prevent the taking in any incorporated city or borough, any dwelling house, &c., necessary and convenient for depots, &c. See ante, p. 13.

SECTION 2. That so much of the eleventh section of the act of Assembly entitled "An Act to incorporate the Pennsylvania Railroad Company," approved April thirteenth, one thousand eight hundred and forty-six, as prohibits the said company from passing through any dwelling-house, shall not be construed so as to prevent the taking in any incorporated city or borough, of any dwelling house by whomsoever possessed or occupied, and the land on which the same is erected, which may be necessary or convenient for depots, warehouses, offices, toll houses, engine and water stations, or other buildings or appurtenances; but the right of said company to take such property for such purposes is hereby declared and affirmed: *Provided*, That full compensation be made to the owner or owners of such buildings, for all damages sustained thereby, the same to be ascertained as in other cases: *Provided*, That the prices heretofore agreed to be paid by said railroad company, and agreed to be received by the owners of property in the city of Pittsburgh, shall not, in any case, be reduced by any decision or decisions of a jury or juries that may be appointed to assess damages: *And provided further*, That the said power of entering upon property, as authorized by this act, shall be limited to that part of the First Ward in said city of Pittsburgh, being between Marbury, Water, Liberty and Penn streets.

Proviso.

Proviso.

Proviso.

Of entry to certain parts of First Ward, Pittsburgh. See Sup. April 21, 1854, post, p. 37.

Approved February 17th, 1854.

A FURTHER SUPPLEMENT

TO THE ACT INCORPORATING THE PENNSYLVANIA RAILROAD COMPANY.

For certain purposes company shall have power to increase their loans, and erect certain buildings, &c. See ante, p. 7.

SECTION 1. That the Pennsylvania Railroad Company, for the purpose of completing their second track, increasing their motive power, and building suitable houses at Philadelphia, Pittsburgh, and along the line of their road, for the reception and accommodation of travelers and the storage of freight, and which they are hereby authorized to erect, shall have power to increase their loans: *Provided*, The debts and other obligations of the company, including loans, shall not at any time exceed the amount of capital stock paid in and expended on the road and its equipment: *Provided further*, That the loans contemplated in this act shall not be made unless with the assent of a majority of the stockholders of said company, represented at a stated or special meeting of the same.

Proviso.

Proviso.

Approved April 18*th*, 1854.

A FURTHER SUPPLEMENT

TO AN ACT INCORPORATING THE PENNSYLVANIA RAILROAD COMPANY, PASSED THE THIRTEENTH DAY OF APRIL, ONE THOUSAND EIGHT HUNDRED AND FORTY-SIX.

Part of act of Feb'y 18, 1854, authorizing entry by company on certain property in Pittsburgh, repealed. See ante, p. 36, sec. 2. Sup. Feb. 17, 1854.

SECTION 1. That so much of an act that became a law on the eighteenth of February, one thousand eight hundred and fifty-four, entitled "A further Supplement to an Act incorporating the Pennsylvania Railroad Company, passed the thirteenth of April, one thousand eight hundred and forty-six," as gives power to said railroad company to enter upon property situated between Marbury, Penn, Water streets and Exchange alley, in the First Ward of the city of Pittsburgh, be and the same is hereby repealed.

Approved April 21*st*, 1854.

A SUPPLEMENT

TO THE ACT INCORPORATING THE PENNSYLVANIA RAILROAD COMPANY.

Board of directors authorized to increase, from time to time, capital stock of company, such increase not to exceed 40,000 shares. Increased 20,000 shares by sec. 4, Act of May 6, 1852, post, p 48. See ante, pp. 17, 33, 34.

Annual election of board of directors, when and where held. Annual meeting of stockholders, when held. See ante. p. 8.

No one eligible as director unless possessed, in his own right, of 50 shares of stock at least 90 days before election. See ante, p. 9.

SECTION 1. That the board of directors of the Pennsylvania Railroad Company shall have authority to increase, from time to time, the capital stock of the company, such increase not to exceed forty thousand shares.

SECTION 2. That the annual election of the board of directors shall hereafter be held at the office of the company, in Philadelphia, between the hours of ten A. M. and six P. M., on the first Monday of March of each year. The annual meeting of the stockholders to be held on the first Monday of February, as heretofore.

SECTION 3. That no person shall be eligible to fill the office of director, who shall not have been possessed, in his own right, of not less than fifty shares of the stock of the company, at least ninety days previous to his election, either by the private stockholders, or by the municipal corporations holding stock in the company; that any vacancies that may hereafter occur in the board, from any cause whatever, shall be filled by the board in the manner provided for in the fifth section of the charter of the company, to which this is a supplement: *Provided*, That before this act shall go into effect, it shall be approved by the stockholders, at a general meeting called for that purpose.

Approved May 2d, 1855.

A FURTHER SUPPLEMENT

TO AN ACT TO INCORPORATE THE PENNSYLVANIA RAILROAD COMPANY, PASSED APRIL THIRTEENTH, ONE THOUSAND EIGHT HUNDRED AND FORTY-SIX.

Company authorized to construct a railroad from the Philadelphia and Columbia railroad, north of Market street, Philadelphia, to Delaware river.

SECTION 1. That the Pennsylvania Railroad Company be and is hereby authorized to construct a railroad from a point on the Philadelphia and Columbia railroad north of Market street, in the city of Philadelphia, near the repair shops of said company; thence passing behind the said shops, across Market street; thence down the centre of Mansiōn street, to the West Chester railroad; thence to some point on the west side of the river Schuylkill, at or near Gray's ferry bridge; thence crossing said river to the river Delaware, and terminating thereon south of the Navy Yard, by such route as may be most practicable and conducive to the public interests: *Provided, however*, That the line of said road from a point one hundred feet north of the north side of Market street to the south side of Chestnut street, and if practicable, further south, shall be by means of a tunnel at such distance below the surface as not to interfere with pipes and culverts, and from the point where said tunnel may terminate, to the south side of Walnut street; said road shall be under the surface by means of a tunnel or covered way, whichever may be most practicable, and from thence to a point one hundred feet further southward, by a covered way under or above the surface, as may be necessary, and on the line of said Mansion street, below Chestnut street, the location of said pipes and culverts may be altered by the board as shall be requisite: *And provided further*, said road shall not pass through any part of the Woodland Cemetery without the consent of the directors thereof, and shall be located, as regards grades and route, with the approval of the board of survey of said city, and subject to such regulations as the Councils of said city may from time to time ordain for the public convenience and safety.

See sec. 3, Act of May 16, 1857, post, p. 64

Proviso.

Proviso.

SECTION 2. That the Councils of said city are hereby authorized to widen to a width not exceeding one hundred feet, any of the streets of said city that may be occupied by the route of said railroad so extended, and to cause the same to be laid out upon the plans of said city, of said increased width, the damages therefor to be ascertained in the manner now provided by law in reference to the opening of the streets of said city: *Provided*, That the said company shall first give security to said city for the payment of all such damages.

Councils authorized to widen streets occupied by route of road as extended, &c.

How damages ascertained.

Proviso.

SECTION 3. That the said company shall have full power and authority to construct at the Delaware and Schuylkill rivers, on or contiguous to the line of said railroad, such area of ground not exceeding, in the aggregate, twenty-five acres, wharves, docks and warehouses, with the necessary appurtenances, as may be required for the proper accommodation of the freight passing over said road, and to charge and collect storage and wharfage at reasonable and customary rates: *Provided, however*, That other parties desiring to make connections with said railroad shall be at liberty to do so under such regulations as may be necessary for safety and convenience: *Provided further*, That all freight and business of what-

Company authorized to construct wharves, &c., on Delaware and Schuylkill rivers, on line of road.

Charge & collect storage, &c.

Proviso.

ever kind carried over the Columbia railroad by the Pennsylvania company, and destined for the city of Philadelphia, or taken therefrom for westward transportation, by said company, shall, whenever requested by the owner or transporter of such freight, be delivered or received in Market street by said company, as heretofore, and any evasion of this proviso shall subject the president and directors, or any other officer or agent assenting thereto, each to a fine of one hundred dollars for every offence, to be recovered as debts of like amount are now recoverable, one-half for the use of the complainant, and the other half for the use of the guardians of the poor of said city.

Penalty for evasion of proviso.

How recovered.

For whose use.

SECTION 4. That the said company be and is hereby authorized and empowered to connect the said railroad with any railroads now or hereafter constructed within the limits of the city of Philadelphia, upon the route of said road so extended, on such terms, and for such time, and under such restrictions, as may be agreed upon by the officers and directors of said companies.

Company authorized to connect said railroad with other railroads in Philadelphia, on route of extended road.

On what terms.

SECTION 5. That before this act shall go into effect it shall be approved by the stockholders at a general meeting to be called for that purpose.

Act not to go into effect until approved by stockholders.

Approved April 18th, 1856.

A FURTHER SUPPLEMENT

TO THE ACT TO INCORPORATE THE PENNSYLVANIA RAILROAD COMPANY.

SECTION 1. That so much of the tenth section of the charter of the said company as requires the payment of a dividend ten days after its declaration, be and the same is hereby repealed; and that each dividend that may hereafter be declared, shall be paid to the stockholders, or their legal representatives, on application at the office of the said company, at any time not exceeding thirty days after its declaration, as the board of directors may fix.

So much of 10th section of charter as requires Company to pay dividends ten days after they are declared repealed, and Company may pay any time within 30 days after they are declared, as directors may fix. Ante, p. 12.

Approved May 21st, 1857.

ACTS OF ASSEMBLY

AFFECTING THE COMPANY.

AN ACT

TO EXEMPT CERTAIN CERTIFICATES OF LOAN FROM TAXATION FOR COUNTY AND MUNICIPAL PURPOSES.

SECTION 1. That the certificates of loan heretofore issued, or which shall hereafter be issued by the county of Allegheny, by the city of Pittsburgh, by the city of Allegheny, or by the city of Philadelphia, in payment of any subscription made by said county or cities, to the capital stock of the Pennsylvania Railroad Company, or the capital stock of the Ohio and Pennsylvania Railroad Company, be and the same are hereby exempted from all taxation within this Commonwealth, except for State purposes.

Certain certificates of loan exempt from taxation except for State purposes.

Approved April 5th, 1849.

A SUPPLEMENT

TO AN ACT ENTITLED "AN ACT TO INCORPORATE THE VILLAGE OF PETERSBURG, IN THE COUNTY OF PERRY, INTO A BOROUGH," PASSED THE TWELFTH DAY OF MARCH, ONE THOUSAND EIGHT HUNDRED AND FORTY-FOUR, &c.

SECTION 6. That the town council of the borough of Petersburg aforesaid, shall have full power and authority to pass such ordinances, and impose and enforce such penalties from time to time, for the protection of the lives and property of the citizens of said borough, as shall effectually prevent the Pennsylvania Central Railroad Company, or their agents, from running their engines and cars through the said borough at a greater speed than eight miles per hour, and to compel them to give due notice, by bell or whistle, before passing any of the cross streets or roads within the limits of said borough.

Borough of Petersburg authorized to pass ordinances and impose penalties, for protection of lives, &c., of citizens, to prevent Pa.R.R. Co. from running engines & cars through borough at greater speed than 8 miles an hour, and compel them to give notice by bell or whistle at crossings.

Approved April 2d, 1850.

AN ACT

TO AUTHORIZE THE COLLECTION OF ROAD TAXES IN CONEMAUGH TOWNSHIP, INDIANA COUNTY, IN MONEY; RELATIVE TO HAWKERS AND PEDLERS IN THE COUNTIES OF ARMSTRONG, INDIANA, BEDFORD, AND CAMBRIA; TO THE ERECTION OF A BRIDGE IN CUMBERLAND COUNTY; TO AUTHORIZE THE PENNSYLVANIA RAILROAD TO CONSTRUCT A LATERAL ROAD IN THE COUNTY OF INDIANA; AND EXTENDING CERTAIN ROAD LAWS IN SUSQUEHANNA COUNTY.

Pennsylvania railroad company authorized to construct a lateral railroad.

SECTION 4. That the Pennsylvania Railroad Company be and is hereby authorized to construct a lateral railroad from a point at or near Liebengood's summit, on the said Pennsylvania Railroad, in Derry Township, Westmoreland county, to a point at or near the borough of Blairsville, in the county of Indiana, subject to the provisions contained in the Act of Assembly incorporating said company, and the various supplements thereto.

Approved April 6th, 1850.

AN ACT

TO INCORPORATE THE SOUTHERN GAS COMPANY, AND RELATIVE TO THE APPRAISERS OF TAVERN LICENSES IN THE CITY AND COUNTY OF PHILADELPHIA.

Subscription by municipal corporations may be by vote of a majority of the commissioners. Subscriptions to be paid in certificates of loan at par. Certificates not to be taxed except for state purposes. Repealed by Act of April 10, 1851, sec. 6, post, p. 45.

SECTION 11. That the authority given to municipal corporations to subscribe to the stock of the Pennsylvania Railroad Company, by the Supplement to an act entitled "An Act to incorporate the Pennsylvania Railroad Company, approved March twenty-seventh, one thousand eight hundred and forty-eight," shall be granted by a majority of the Board of Commissioners of the several districts therein referred to, provided said railroad company will take in payment of such subscriptions the certificates of loan of said corporations at par, which certificates shall be exempt from taxation, except for State purposes.

Approved May 15th, 1850.

AN ACT

TO AMEND AN ACT ENTITLED "AN ACT TO INCORPORATE THE MARSHALL SAVING ASSOCIATION OF THE CITY AND COUNTY OF PHILADELPHIA," APPROVED THE TWENTY-SECOND DAY OF MARCH, ONE THOUSAND EIGHT HUNDRED AND FIFTY, AND RELATIVE TO THE ESTATES OF SARAH KNORR AND THOMAS REEVES, AND IN REFERENCE TO DEEDS AND THE COLLECTORS OF CORPORATION TAXES IN THE DISTRICT OF THE NORTHERN LIBERTIES, IN THE COUNTY OF PHILADELPHIA.

SECTION 6. That the eleventh section of an act entitled "An Act to incorporate the Southern Gas Company, and relative to the appraisers of tavern licenses in the city and county of Philadelphia," approved the fifteenth day of May, one thousand eight hundred and fifty, be and the same is hereby repealed.

Pennsylvania Railroad Company, repeal of certain act concerning. Ante, p. 44.

Approved April 10th, 1851.

AN ACT

CONSTRUING THE FIFTH SECTION OF THE ACT ENTITLED "A FURTHER SUPPLEMENT TO AN ACT TO INCORPORATE THE PENNSYLVANIA RAILROAD COMPANY," AND RELATIVE TO THE OBSTRUCTION OF PRIVATE ROADS BY RAILROAD COMPANIES; RELATIVE TO HOLDING ELECTIONS IN SPARTA TOWNSHIP, CRAWFORD COUNTY, AND THE BOROUGH OF LORETTO, CAMBRIA COUNTY; AUTHORIZING JOHN McDILL TO SELL CERTAIN REAL ESTATE; TO A VOLUNTEER COMPANY CALLED THE BROAD TOP RIFLE RANGERS; TO THE BOROUGH OF EBENSBURG, CAMBRIA COUNTY; TO SUPERVISORS IN LANCASTER AND JEFFERSON COUNTIES; CHANGING THE NAME OF THE NORTHUMBERLAND AND POINT INFANTRY, A VOLUNTEER COMPANY; TO THE CHESTNUT HILL IRON ORE COMPANY; TO AN ELECTION DISTRICT IN CLEARFIELD COUNTY, AND TO THE CONOCOCHEAGUE CREEK IN FRANKLIN COUNTY.

SECTION 1. That the fifth section of the act entitled "A further supplement to An Act to incorporate the Pennsylvania Railroad Company," passed the twenty-eighth day of March, one thousand eight hundred and forty-eight, shall be so construed as to include the streets, lanes and alleys, in any town, borough or city through which said road passes.

Construing fifth section of certain act relative to the Pennsylvania Railroad. Ante, p. 29.

Relative to the obstruction of private roads by railroad companies.

SECTION 2. That any chartered railroad company in this Commonwealth obstructing or impeding the free use or passage of any private road or crossing place, by standing burthen cars or engines, or placing other obstructions on any railroad wherever any private road or crossing place may be necessary to enable the occupant or occupants of lands or farms to pass over any railroad with horses, cows, hogs, sheep, carts, wagons, and implements of husbandry, shall for every such offence, after any agent or other person in the employment of any railroad company shall have received at least fifteen minutes' verbal notice to remove burthen cars, engines, or other obstructions, from any private road or crossing place, that may pass over any railroad, be liable for a penalty of thirty dollars, which shall be for the use of the person or persons aggrieved, and which shall be recovered before any justice of the peace in the same manner that debts not exceeding one hundred dollars are by law recoverable. And in all suits or actions that may be brought against any railroad company for the recovery of said penalty of thirty dollars, the service of legal process on any agent or other person in the employment of any railroad company shall be as good and available in law as if made on the president thereof.

Approved April 12th, 1851.

AN ACT

TO AUTHORIZE THE PENNSYLVANIA RAILROAD COMPANY TO EXTEND ITS LATERAL ROAD NOW MADE FROM LIEBENGOOD'S SUMMIT IN WESTMORELAND COUNTY TO THE BOROUGH OF BLAIRSVILLE, TO THE BOROUGH OF INDIANA, IN THE COUNTY OF INDIANA.

SECTION 1. That the Pennsylvania Railroad Company be, and is hereby authorized, if they deem it expedient, to extend its lateral road now made from Leibengood's Summit, in Westmoreland county to the borough of Blairsville, in a northerly direction, to the borough of Indiana, in the county of Indiana; and that hereafter the said lateral road shall be subject to all the provisions of the several acts of Assembly relating to the said Pennsylvania Railroad, excepting the toll on tonnage provided for in the twenty-second section of the act of thirteenth of April, one thousand eight hundred and forty-six, entitled "An Act to incorporate the Pennsylvania Railroad Company."

Approved January 29th, 1852.

AN ACT

AUTHORIZING THE PENNSYLVANIA RAILROAD COMPANY TO CONSTRUCT A LATERAL RAILROAD FROM THEIR MAIN ROAD IN WESTMORELAND COUNTY, TO UNIONTOWN, IN FAYETTE COUNTY, WITH POWER TO EXTEND THE SAME TO GENEVA, IN SAID COUNTY.

Pennsylvania Railroad Company authorized to construct lateral railroad to Uniontown.

SECTION 1. That the Pennsylvania Railroad Company be, and is hereby authorized, if they deem it expedient, to construct a lateral railroad from some point on the Pennsylvania Railroad, between the borough of Greensburg and the town of Latrobe, in Westmoreland county, in a southern direction, by way of or near Mount Pleasant, in Westmoreland county, and Connellsville, in Fayette county, to the borough of Uniontown, in Fayette county, and that hereafter the said lateral road shall be subject to all the provisions of the several acts of Assembly relating to the said Pennsylvania Railroad Company, excepting the toll on tonnage, provided for in the twenty-second section of the act of the thirteenth of April, one thousand eight hundred and forty-six, entitled "An Act to incorporate the Pennsylvania Railroad Company."

Extension of lateral road to Geneva.

SECTION 2. That the said Pennsylvania Railroad Company shall also have the privilege, and they are hereby authorized, after the said lateral road shall have been completed and in operation, to extend the said lateral road from Uniontown to or near the town of Geneva, or some other point on or near the waters of the Monongahela, in said county of Fayette, or to the borough of Waynesburg, in Greene county, as may be deemed most expedient and advantageous by said company, subject to the like provisions and restrictions as are imposed in the preceding section of this act, on the proposed lateral road from the main stem of the Pennsylvania Railroad to Uniontown.

Approved February 28th, 1852.

AN ACT

RELATING TO THE DISTRICT OF WEST PHILADELPHIA; AND TO CHANGE THE NAME OF JOSEPH PARRISH TO JOSEPH AUSTIN PARRISH; RELATIVE TO THE COMMISSIONERS OF THE DISTRICT OF KENSINGTON; AND TO STREETS IN MOYAMENSING; TO CERTIFICATES OF LOAN OF THE PENNSYLVANIA RAILROAD COMPANY; TO THE CHESTNUT HILL RAILROAD COMPANY; AND TO NOTARIES PUBLIC IN PHILADELPHIA.

Certificates of loan of Pennsylvania Railroad Co. subject to taxation.

SECTION 6. That all certificates of loan of the Pennsylvania Railroad Company shall be subject to taxation for State purposes only, as is now provided by law in the case of certificates of loan received by said company in payment of subscriptions to its capital stock made by municipal corporations.

Approved May 1st, 1852.

AN ACT

TO INCORPORATE THE MANOR TURNPIKE AND PLANK ROAD COMPANY; TO INCREASE THE CAPITAL STOCK OF THE PENNSYLVANIA RAILROAD COMPANY.

Pennsylvania railroad company to issue additional shares of stock. See ante, pp. 6, 17, 33, 34, 38. See Act of May 16, 1857, sec. 3, post, p. 62.

SECTION 4. That it shall be lawful for the Pennsylvania Railroad Company, in addition to the capital stock authorized by the twentieth section of an act incorporating the said company, passed the thirteenth day of April, one thousand eight hundred and forty-six, and any supplement thereto, to issue certificates for any additional sum not exceeding twenty thousand shares, and to demand and receive the moneys for said additional shares when subscribed for, in like manner and upon the same conditions as to instalments and otherwise, as are provided for in the ninth section of the said original act: *Provided*, The par value of said additional capital stock shall be fifty dollars per share as heretofore, and that the holders thereof shall have all the rights and immunities which by law are invested in the subscribers to the capital stock originally authorized to be created.

Approved May 6th, 1852.

AN ACT

AUTHORIZING THE COMMISSIONERS OF FAYETTE COUNTY AND THE BOROUGHS OF UNIONTOWN AND CONNELLSVILLE, IN SAID COUNTY, AND THE BOROUGHS OF MOUNT PLEASANT AND YOUNGSTOWN, IN WESTMORELAND COUNTY, TO SUBSCRIBE TO THE CAPITAL STOCK OF THE PENNSYLVANIA RAILROAD COMPANY.

SECTION 1. That the borough of Uniontown and the boroughs of Connellsville, in the county of Fayette, and the boroughs of Mount Pleasant and Youngstown, in Westmoreland county, are hereby authorized and empowered to subscribe for shares in the capital stock of the Pennsylvania Railroad, to be applied to the construction of the Uniontown branch, not exceeding two thousand shares each, and to borrow money to pay therefor, and to make provision for the payment of the principal and interest of the money so borrowed, by the assessment and collection of such taxes as may be necessary for that purpose, and also, as in other cases of loans to corporations; and no certificate of loan or bond shall be issued by said corporations for a less sum than one hundred dollars, and shall be transferable as shall be directed by said corporations respectively; and the certificates of loans or bonds to be issued by either of the said corporations for the purpose aforesaid, bearing a rate of interest not exceeding six per centum per annum, payable half yearly, may be received by said Pennsylvania Railroad Company, in payment of instalments on shares subscribed by said corporations, in such terms as shall be agreed upon between said company and said corporations. Certain boroughs authorized to subscribe stock to Pennsylvania railroad.

SECTION 2. That the subscription of stock aforesaid shall be directed by resolution passed by the corporate constituted authorities of said boroughs respectively, and said corporations may be represented at elections and other meetings of said railroad company by agents duly authorized by resolutions of the constituted authorities thereof. Subscriptions, how directed.

SECTION 3. That the commissioners of the county of Fayette, or a majority of them, be and they are hereby authorized and empowered to subscribe for shares in the capital stock of the Pennsylvania Railroad Company, to be applied to the construction of the Uniontown branch, not exceeding five thousand shares, in the name and behalf of said county, and to borrow money to pay therefor, and to make provision for the payment of the principal and interest Commissioners of Fayette county authorized to subscribe stock.

of the money so borrowed, as in other cases of loans to corporations: *Provided*, That before any such subscription is made, the amount thereof shall be fixed and determined by the grand jury of said county, and upon the report of such grand jury being filed, it shall be lawful for the county commissioners to carry the same into effect by making, in the name of the county, the subscription so directed by said grand inquest: *Provided further*, That whenever bonds of the county are given in payment of subscription, the same shall not be sold by said railroad company at less than par value, and no bonds shall be in less amount than one hundred dollars: *And provided further*, That such bonds shall not be subject to taxation until the clear profits of the road shall amount to six per centum upon the cost thereof.

Proviso. Proviso. Proviso.

Certificates of loan.

SECTION 4. That the commissioners of said county, or a majority of them, may issue certificates of loan or bonds in the name of said county, redeemable in not less than ten nor more than twenty-five years, bearing a rate of interest not exceeding six per centum per annum, payable semi-annually, which shall be transferable as may be directed by said commissioners, or a majority of them, and the said certificates of loan or bonds may be received in payment of instalments on shares of stock subscribed for said county, upon such terms as may be agreed upon by said company and the commissioners aforesaid, and the said county may be represented at elections and other meetings of said company, by agents duly authorized and appointed by resolutions of the board of commissioners of said county.

Approved May 1st, 1853.

AN ACT

AUTHORIZING THE PENNSYLVANIA RAILROAD COMPANY TO RUN THEIR CARS OVER CONNECTING AND CONTINUOUS RAILROADS.

SECTION 1. That the Pennsylvania Railroad Company be, and they are hereby authorized to run their cars and locomotives over all connecting and continuous railroads, with the consent of the companies owning the same, and also, their cars over the railroads belonging to this commonwealth, for the transportation of freight, [passengers, their baggage, and the United States mails,*] with the right of attachment to the motive power of the State, employed for these respective purposes, upon such terms and conditions as may be agreed upon between the canal commissioners and said Pennsylvania Railroad Company, or in case of failure to agree, then upon terms and conditions that shall not be less favorable to said company than those that may be established from time to time, by the canal commissioners, for the government of individuals doing business on said railroads, except those engaged in the transportation of freight passing the whole distance between Philadelphia and Pittsburgh, over the public works: *Provided*, That nothing herein contained shall be so construed as to affect or impair the contract made with Bingham and Dock, for the transportation of passengers and mails over the Philadelphia and Columbia railroad by said commissioners, which contract is hereby confirmed: *Provided*, That the Legislature hereby reserves the right to repeal this act of Assembly, in such manner, however, that no injustice shall be done to the parties: *And provided*, That the canal commissioners shall at all times be required to run a sufficient number of engines between Lancaster and Philadelphia, to accommodate the local and way freight.

Approved March 3d, 1853.

AN ACT

TO AUTHORIZE THE BOROUGH OF GREENSBURG TO SUBSCRIBE TO THE CAPITAL STOCK OF THE PENNSYLVANIA RAILROAD COMPANY; RELATIVE TO VACANCIES IN THE BOARD OF DIRECTORS OF ROAD COMPANIES IN ALLEGHENY COUNTY; TO BOROUGH OFFICERS IN PORT CLINTON, SCHUYLKILL COUNTY; RELATING TO THE PROTHONOTARY OF WESTMORELAND COUNTY; RELATIVE TO THE MANOR TURNPIKE AND PLANK ROAD; AND REPEALING THE ACT AUTHORIZING THE SALE OF THE WARREN BRIDGE; AND RELATING TO OVERSEERS OF THE POOR AND SUPERVISORS OF THE SEVERAL TOWNSHIPS IN ALLEGHENY COUNTY.

Borough of Greensburg to subscribe to the capital stock of the Pennsylvania Railroad Co.

SECTION 1. That the burgesses of the borough of Greensburg, in the county of Westmoreland, be and they are hereby authorized and empowered to subscribe, not exceeding one thousand shares, to the capital stock of the Pennsylvania Railroad Company, for the pur-

---

* Repealed by Act of May 13th, 1856. Vide post, page 60.

pose of constructing a branch of said railroad from a point on said road at or near said borough to the borough of Uniontown, in Fayette county; and the said burgesses are hereby further authorized and empowered to issue bonds of the said borough of Greensburg, to the amount subscribed as aforesaid, bearing interest not exceeding six per centum per annum, payable semi-annually, the principal whereof shall be payable at a period not exceeding twenty years, which said bonds may be received by the Pennsylvania Railroad Company, in payment of the stock subscribed as aforesaid, and not to be issued for sums less than one hundred dollars, and assignable only upon the book or books provided by said burgesses for that purpose, by the holders thereof or their heirs or legal representatives, or by some person having a power of attorney to make such assignment:

Proviso. *Provided*, That the said bonds shall not be issued as aforesaid until the taxable inhabitants of said borough shall first approve of the subscription aforesaid, at an election to be called and held for that purpose by the burgesses of said borough, and to be conducted according to such rules as the said burgesses shall establish.

Approved March 19th, 1853.

AN ACT

TO INCORPORATE THE WOODBURY AND BROAD TOP TURNPIKE OR PLANK ROAD COMPANY; RELATIVE TO SALE OF A SCHOOL HOUSE IN FULTON COUNTY; EXTENDING THE PROVISIONS OF THE SECOND SECTION OF THE ACT REGULATING BOROUGHS TO THE BOROUGH OF PINE GROVE, SCHUYLKILL COUNTY; EXTENDING THE PROVISIONS OF THE ACT TO ENCOURAGE MANUFACTURING OPERATIONS TO THE MANUFACTURE OF FLOUR AND MEAL, IN THE COUNTIES OF PHILADELPHIA AND BEAVER; TO THE WILL OF JACOB MOYER, DECEASED, OF BEDFORD COUNTY; TO PROHIBIT THE KEEPING OF BAGATELLE ROOMS IN ALLEGHENY COUNTY; RELATIVE TO THE MILL-DAM OF M. M'CULLOUGH, OF ALLEGHENY COUNTY; AUTHORIZING THE PENNSYLVANIA RAILROAD COMPANY TO CONSTRUCT A LINE OF TELEGRAPH ALONG THEIR ROAD; AND REFUNDING CERTAIN MONEY TO WUNDERLICH AND NEAD, OF FRANKLIN COUNTY.

Penna. railroad company authorized to construct a line of telegraph.

SECTION 18. That the Pennsylvania Railroad Company be and they are hereby authorized to make and construct a line of telegraph wires along and adjacent to the line of their railroad, from the city of Pittsburg to Harrisburg, and from Harrisburg, connecting with the former, to the city of Philadelphia, along and adjacent to the line of the Harrisburg and Lancaster, and Philadelphia and Columbia Railroads; and for the purpose of making, erecting and constructing the same, the said company or their agents are hereby authorized to enter and go upon the premises of any person or persons, and erect posts, and use any tree for the purpose of suspending their wires, and construct the same: *Provided*, The said company shall not erect posts for the reception of said wires more than five feet from the tracks of said railroads, without the consent of the owner or owners of the land through which said railroads pass, nor shall they cut down or destroy trees or other property, without tendering full compensation therefor, and to make and use branches from the main line to any of their stations, and to use the same for telegraphic communication, for themselves and the use of the company, and to enter at any time upon the property on which their said line is constructed for general or special repair of any part or all of their said line, and to suspend their wires on any part of the public improvements along said line; and in case of damage done to any individual, they may be sued for the same in any of the courts of this Commonwealth, for the damage actually sustained; *Provided*, That the consent of the Canal Commissioners be first had. Proviso.

Proviso.

Approved May 11th, 1853.

AN ACT

TO AUTHORIZE WILLIAM C. PATTERSON AND OTHERS TO CONVEY THE POWELTON ESTATE IN WEST PHILADELPHIA,

Preamble.

WHEREAS, William C. Patterson, Samuel V. Merrick, David S. Brown, Thomas T. Lea, Alexander J. Derbyshire, Washington Butcher, and Edward M. Davis, have taken as purchasers thereof a conveyance of the whole estate called Powelton, on the west side of the Schuylkill river, in the county of Philadelphia, in order to secure what they deemed only necessary conveniences for the proper business of the Pennsylvania Railroad Company, in West Philadelphia, and the said company have no authority by law to hold more than thirty acres of said estate, and the same being burdensome to the said purchasers to hold as individuals; Therefore,

Purchasers authorized to convey Powelton

SECTION 1. *Be it enacted, &c.*, That authority is hereby given to the said purchasers to convey the said estate, or the residue thereof, estate to trustees of Pa. R. R. Company.

being about sixty-two acres, more or less, in extent, to any trustee or trustees who may be selected or approved by the board of directors of said company, in fee simple, and the said trustee or trustees to whom the said estate, or the residue thereof, shall be conveyed, and the successor or successors of the said trustee or trustees, duly appointed, shall have full power and authority to hold the same for the use and benefit of the said the Pennsylvania Railroad Company, for and during the term of five years from the first day of July, one thousand eight hundred and fifty-three, for the purpose of selling and conveying the same, or any part or parts thereof, to any person or persons, according to the orders of the said Pennsylvania Railroad Company, and account to the said corporation for the proceeds of such sale or sales, and in the meantime, until such sale or sales shall be effected, to permit and suffer such use and uses of the said estate, or any part or parts thereof, as the said Pennsylvania Railroad Company or their board of directors may order and direct, and the said Pennsylvania Railroad Company is hereby authorized to indemnify the purchasers aforesaid named in the preamble, against any loss which may accrue from the sale of said remainder of the Powelton estate.

Trustees may sell and convey estate or apply to other uses. See Act of April 22, 1856, post, p. 58, and Act of April 1, 1858, post, p. 73.

Approved May 20th, 1853.

AN ACT

TO AUTHORIZE THE PENNSYLVANIA RAILROAD COMPANY TO MAKE CONNECTIONS TO AND FROM THEIR FREIGHT DEPOT, IN THE CITY OF PHILADELPHIA.

Company authorized to make tracks from their freight depot in Philadelphia, along certain streets, to connect with railroad on Market and Broad sts.

SECTION 1. That the Pennsylvania Railroad Company be and they are hereby authorized to make such connection from their freight depot, in the city of Philadelphia, by laying a track or tracks of railway from said depot along Juniper street to Market street, and along Olive street to Broad street, to connect with the railroad on said Market and Broad streets respectively, with such extension along the said Juniper street to or beyond Kelly street as may be necessary and convenient for the accommodation of cars and the transaction of their business of transportation: *Provided*, That the consent and approbation of the Select and Common Councils of the city of Philadelphia first be had in writing; and if constructed, the laying of such track or tracks shall be subject to the control and direction of said Councils, or their deputed agent or agents.

Proviso.

Approved February 16th, 1854.

AN ACT

AUTHORIZING THE COUNCILS OF THE CITY OF PITTSBURGH TO OPEN PART OF FERGUSON STREET AND TO CLOSE BELL'S ALLEY.

Ordinance of Councils changing course, &c., of Ferguson st., Pittsburgh, and vacating Bell's alley, Pittsburgh, confirmed, and title to any street or alley so vacated confirmed to Pa. R. R. Co.

SECTION 1. *Be it enacted, &c.*, That any ordinance passed or to be passed by the Select and Common Councils of the city of Pittsburgh, for changing part of the course of Ferguson street, and vacating and opening the same, and any such ordinance for vacating and closing Bell's alley, or any part thereof, is hereby allowed, ratified and confirmed in such manner as to make the opening, changing, vacating and closing aforesaid, legal and valid, and the title to any street or alley so vacated is hereby confirmed to the Pennsylvania Railroad Company, so long as they are owners of the adjoining property.

Approved April 19th, 1854.

AN ACT

AUTHORIZING THE OPENING OF A STREET IN THE CITY OF PITTSBURGH.

Preamble.

WHEREAS, The city of Pittsburgh did, by ordinance of the Councils of said city enacted on the twenty-eighth day of July, one thousand eight hundred and fifty-three, among other things, vacate and consent to the vacation of so much of Ferguson street, in the said city, as lies between a point on said street five hundred and fifty feet east from the eastern line of Lumber street and Morton street, and did give exclusive occupancy and use thereof to the Pennsylvania Railroad Company: *Provided*, That the said company should, at its own cost, cause to be laid out and graded along the south line of the southern track of said railroad, and parallel to and adjoining therewith a space or street of forty feet in width, extending the length of that part of Ferguson street vacated and connecting therewith;

And whereas, The said company has no power to take and appropriate the strip of land necessary for the opening of said space or street;

Powers, &c., of Pa. R. R. Co. to appropriate land extended to embrace a strip extending the length of that part of Ferguson street, Pittsburgh, vacated and connecting therewith.

SECTION 1. *Be it enacted, &c.,* That all the rights, powers, privileges and proceedings provided for by any existing law by which the Pennsylvania Railroad Company may appropriate land for the necessary route of the road, or any other purposes connected therewith, be and they are hereby extended to and so as to embrace the said space or street of forty feet in width, extending the length of that part of Ferguson street vacated by the ordinance of the city of Pittsburgh of July twenty-eighth, one thousand eight hundred and fifty-three: *Provided,* That compensation be made to the owners of any property which may be taken for said space or street, in the manner now provided by law for the ascertaining of the damage arising from the taking of land for the necessary route of the road, or other purposes connected therewith; and in estimating said question of damage, the viewers shall make a fair and just comparison of the advantages and disadvantages, and consider and determine whether upon the whole the taking of the said land is or is not an injury, and award and report accordingly: *Provided also,* That when the proceedings are completed, the ground so to be taken shall be forever a public highway and one of the streets of the city of Pittsburgh, like all other streets in said city: *Provided further,* That the viewers appointed in this case shall be residents of the county of Allegheny: *And provided further,* That this act shall not be construed to affect any portion of said Ferguson street lying east of Morton street.

(Margin: Proviso. Proviso. Proviso. Proviso.)

Approved April 6th, 1855.

AN ACT

EXEMPTING COAL AND LUMBER FROM THE TONNAGE TAX.

SECTION 1. That the several acts imposing a tax on tonnage passing over the Pennsylvania Railroad, and the Harrisburg, Lancaster and Mount Joy Railroad, shall not hereafter apply to lumber or coal: *Provided,* That said companies shall made a permanent deduction from their rates of charges on said articles below their schedule rates for goods now or hereafter to be embraced in the same class, equal to or greater than said tax: *And provided further,* That the legislature reserves the right to repeal this act at any time, and to re-enact the several acts hereby repealed.

(Margin: Proviso. Proviso.)

Approved May 7th, 1855.

AN ACT

TO AUTHORIZE THE PENNSYLVANIA RAILROAD COMPANY TO PURCHASE AND HOLD CERTAIN REAL ESTATE IN THE CITY OF PITTSBURGH.

WHEREAS, an agreement was made on the twenty-second day of February, one thousand eight hundred and fifty-four, for the purchase by said company of a certain lot of ground on Liberty street, in the city of Pittsburgh, on which was erected Saint Patrick's Roman Catholic Church, and part of which was used as a burying ground; *and whereas*, it has become necessary for the vesting of an indisputable title to said lot, that the Legislature shall authorize proceedings to this end, now, for the quieting of all such doubts, and to enable the company to take and hold said property: Preamble.

SECTION 1. That the Pennsylvania Railroad Company shall have the right, by the true intent and meaning of their charter and the several supplements thereto, to appropriate, hold, and use the said described lot of ground, with the appurtenances, and to erect and establish depots and warehouses thereon, in like manner and to the same extent as if the route of the road itself, and so much of the said charter and supplements thereto as prohibit them from so appropriating any burying ground or place of public worship, be and the same is hereby repealed, so far as is concerned the lot of ground on Liberty street, in the city of Pittsburgh, lately used for Saint Patrick's Roman Catholic Church and burying ground: *Provided*, That no entry shall be actually made on said ground, until the bodies interred therein shall have been removed under the sanction of the Roman Catholic Bishop of Pittsburgh: *And provided further*, That the compensation to be paid by said company, for said premises, shall be paid to the trustee now in possession of said premises, to be by him held and applied, upon the same trusts wherewith said premises are charged; and upon such payment to the trustee aforesaid, the said railroad company shall be discharged from all liability in respect to the application thereof, and shall hold the said premises free and discharged of all trusts whatever.

Company authorized to appropriate, hold and use lot of ground described in preamble, and erect depots, &c., thereon.

Proviso.

Proviso.

Approved February 7th, 1856.

AN ACT

RELATING TO REAL ESTATE HELD BY OR FOR THE PENNSYLVANIA RAILROAD COMPANY.

Company authorized to sell a certain portion of Powelton estate, Philadelphia, in parts, in fee, on ground rent or otherwise, free from the objects of conveyance to them, and to hold the rents reserved. See Act of May 20, 1853, ante, p. 53; and Act of April 1, 1858, post, p. 73.

SECTION 1. That the Pennsylvania Railroad Company be and they are hereby authorized and empowered to sell and dispose of such parts and portions as they may deem expedient, of a certain tract of land situate in the late District of West Philadelphia, now in the consolidated city of Philadelphia, part of the Powelton estate, containing thirty acres, more or less, (which John Hare Powel, by indenture dated the second day of May, Anno Domini eighteen hundred and fifty-three, recorded at Philadelphia, in deed book T. H., number eighty-four, page seventy-three, et cetera, granted unto the said company for the purposes and objects appertaining to the legitimate business of the said company,) and they are hereby authorized to sell, grant and convey the same unto the purchaser or purchasers thereof, in fee simple, upon ground rent or otherwise, free from the purposes and objects aforesaid; and in case any such sale or sales be made in consideration of a yearly rent or rents to be reserved to the said company and to remain charged upon the land so sold, then the said company are hereby authorized to hold and stand seised of such yearly rent or rents, with the rights, incidents and appurtenances thereto belonging, and to sell and dispose of the same when they may deem it expedient: *Provided*, That the said company shall sell and dispose of, absolutely, any ground rent or mortgage arising from the sale of said property, within the period of ten years from the date of its creation.

Proviso.

Company authorized to take from Girard Life Ins. An. and Trust Co. a conveyance in fee of certain parts of Powelton estate.

SECTION 2. That the Pennsylvania Railroad Company aforesaid be and they are hereby authorized and empowered to take and receive from the Girard Life Insurance, Annuity and Trust Company, of Philadelphia, a conveyance of such part or parts as may be suitable to them for the purposes and objects of their incorporation, of a certain tract or parcel of land, also part of the Powelton estate, in West Philadelphia, which William C. Patterson and wife and others, by indenture dated the twenty-first November, Anno Domini one thousand eight hundred and fifty-three, recorded in deed book T. H., number one hundred and one, page five hundred and forty-seven, et cetera, granted unto the Girard Life Insurance, Annuity and Trust Company, of Philadelphia, in trust for certain purposes therein mentioned; and the said land so to be conveyed to the Pennsylvania Railroad Company shall be held by them, their successors and assigns, in fee simple, for the like and same purposes and objects as those for which they have heretofore held the said tract of thirty acres: *Provided*, That the said land so to be conveyed, together with the part of said thirty acres to be retained by the said company, shall not in the whole exceed fifty acres, to be designated or located by the President of the company and the President of the Board of Canal Commissioners: *And provided further*, That the Canal Commissioners are hereby authorized to locate on the north-east side of the Columbia railroad, a piece of land sixty-six feet in width on the surface, with the necessary slope of embankment, from the outside rail of the northern main track, beginning at the southern line of the ground occupied by the Commonwealth for an engine depot, and extending parallel with said railroad to the river Schuylkill, or such portion of said ground as they may deem necessary for the interest of the State, to be paid for at a rate not exceeding the present value thereof.

Proviso.

By whom located.

Proviso.

SECTION 3. *And whereas* the tract of land, part of the Powelton estate in West Philadelphia aforesaid, was conveyed by William C. Patterson and wife, and others, by the above recited indenture to the Girard Life Insurance, Annuity and Trust Company of Philadelphia, their successors and assigns, in trust for the use and benefit of the Pennsylvania Railroad Company, for and during the term of five years from the first day of July, Anno Domini one thousand eight hundred and fifty-three, for the purpose of selling and conveying the same agreeably to an Act of Assembly, number three hundred and seventy-seven, approved on the twentieth of May, one thousand eight hundred and fifty-three: That the said term of five years, limited by the above mentioned Act of Assembly, be and the same is hereby extended to the term of seven years from the said first day of July, one thousand eight hundred and fifty-three; and that the said the Girard Life Insurance, Annuity and Trust Company of Philadelphia, and their successors, shall have full power and authority to hold the said land for the use and benefit of the said Pennsylvania Railroad Company, for and during the term of seven years from the first day of July, one thousand eight hundred and fifty-three, for the purpose of selling and conveying the same or any part thereof to any person or persons in fee simple upon ground rent or otherwise, according to the orders of the said Railroad Company, and in the way and manner directed by the Act of Assembly aforesaid, and set forth in the said last recited indenture.

Preamble.

Limitation of trust to sell said land extended to seven years from July 1, 1853.

Power to Girard Life and Insurance and Trust Company to sell, confirmed.

Approved April 22d, 1856.

A FURTHER SUPPLEMENT

TO THE ACT CONSOLIDATING THE CITY OF PHILADELPHIA.

Chief Engineer and Surveyor of Philadelphia authorized and directed to change grades of certain sts. in said city.

SECTION 18. That the Chief Engineer and Surveyor of the City of Philadelphia be and he is hereby authorized and directed to revise and change the grades of the streets laid out in the Twenty-fourth Ward of said city, north of Market street, the Lancaster Turnpike and south of Bridge street, and east of late Sixth, now Thirty-fifth street, so as to conform, in as great a degree as he shall deem advisable, to the natural grade or surface of the ground; the said revised survey shall be confirmed by the Board of Survey, and be approved by the Court of Quarter Sessions in the manner now provided by law: *Provided*, That no alteration shall be made in the grades of Market street, Lancaster Turnpike, Bridge street, and Sixth street, now Twenty-fourth street as aforesaid; and the Commissioners for the survey of the plan of Blockley, shall proceed to cause the same to be completed and approved by the court, in manner provided by law before said township was embraced in the city of Philadelphia.

Revised survey to be confirmed by Board of Survey and approved by Court of Quarter Sessions.

Proviso.

Approved May 13th, 1856.

AN ACT

TO PROVIDE FOR THE ORDINARY EXPENSES OF GOVERNMENT, THE REPAIRS OF THE PUBLIC CANALS AND RAILROADS, AND OTHER GENERAL AND SPECIAL APPROPRIATIONS.

Repeal of Act of 3d March, 1853, (ante, p. 51.)

SECTION 41. That so much of the act entitled "An act authorizing the Pennsylvania Railroad Company to run their cars over connecting and continuous railroads," approved the third day of March, one thousand eight hundred and fifty-three, as relates to carrying passengers and baggage and mails on the Philadelphia and Columbia railroad, be and the same is hereby repealed; and the canal commissioners are hereby authorized to contract with responsible persons, or companies incorporated by any law of this commonwealth, for carrying passengers, their baggage, and United States mails, on

Canal Commissioners authorized to contract for carrying passengers, &c., over Columbia railroad.

the Philadelphia and Columbia railroad, for a period not exceeding five years from and after the expiration of the contract now existing between the canal commissioners and Bingham & Dock, on such terms and conditions as will best promote the interest of the commonwealth: *Provided*, That from and after the first day of May next it shall not be lawful for the city of Philadelphia to charge and collect tolls on the city railroad for any greater distance than that actually used, including the bridge over the Schuylkill river, at Market street.

Proviso—City of Philadelphia not to charge and collect tolls on city railroads for greater distance than actually used, including Market street bridge.

Approved May 13th, 1856.

AN ACT

RELATING TO THE PENNSYLVANIA RAILROAD COMPANY.

Charter extended for ten years (See ante, p. 21.)

SECTION 1. That the several provisions of the act to incorporate the Pennsylvania Railroad Company, approved the thirteenth day of April, one thousand eight hundred and forty-six, and the supplements thereto, be and the same are hereby extended for the term of ten years from the passage of this act; and all acts and things done by said company, or its agents, since the thirteenth day of April, one thousand eight hundred and fifty-six, are hereby ratified and confirmed, with the same force and effect as if the limitation in the twenty-fifth section of said original act of incorporation had never been imposed.

Approved April 16th, 1857.

AN ACT

FOR THE SALE OF THE MAIN LINE OF THE PUBLIC WORKS.

Notice to be given by the governor, of time and place of sale of main line.

SECTION 1. That it shall be the duty of the governor, within ten days after approving this act, to cause to be advertised daily until the day of sale, in one or more newspapers of extensive circulation, published in the cities of Philadelphia, Pittsburgh, Washington, Boston, New York, and in the borough of Harrisburg, a notice that the main line of the public works will be exposed to public sale, at the Merchants' Exchange, or some other public place in the city of Philadelphia, on a day to be selected by him, not more than forty days after the passage of this act; if a sale shall not be effected on the day fixed by the governor, it shall be lawful for him to adjourn the sale from time to time as he may deem expedient: *Provided*, That public notice of such adjournment shall be given in such newspapers as he may select: *And provided further*, That the last day fixed by adjournment for said sale shall not be less than twenty days before the meeting of the next Legislature.

Proviso.

Proviso.

Main line to be offered.

SECTION 2. That at the time and place so selected, it shall be the duty of the governor to have offered at public sale the whole main line of the public works, to wit: the Philadelphia and Columbia railroad; the canal from Columbia to the Junction at Duncan's Island; the Juniata canal from thence to Hollidaysburgh; the Allegheny Portage railroad, including the new road to avoid the inclined planes, and the canal from Johnstown to Pittsburgh, with all the property thereto appertaining, or in anywise connected therewith.

Who may purchase.

Minimum price.

Purchasers may resell.

SECTION 3. That it shall be lawful for any person or persons, or railroad or canal company now incorporated, or which may hereafter be incorporated by and under the laws of this Commonwealth, to become the purchasers of the said main line of the public works, for any sum not less than seven and a half millions of dollars; and in the event of a sale of the said main line being made to individuals, it shall be lawful for such individuals so purchasing, after the said public sale, to assign and transfer their right to the said main line under said purchase, to any railroad or canal company created by the laws of this Commonwealth; and such railroad or canal company, on compliance with the conditions of the said sale, and on the payment or securing of the purchase money of the said main line to the Commonwealth, as hereinafter provided, shall be fully invested with the right of the said purchasers, and be entitled to the same rights and privileges as if the said main line had been struck off and sold to said company at the time of said public sale, and if necessary, said company may increase their capital stock or borrow money and issue their bonds to any amount not exceeding fifty per centum above the amount of the purchase money; and should any association of individuals become the purchasers of the said main line on the terms prescribed by this act, the governor is hereby authorized to grant them letters patent incorporating the same into a body corporate, in deed and in law, under the name, style and title of the Philadel-

Company purchasing may increase their capital or borrow money.

Letters patent.

Style.

phia and Pittsburg Railroad and Canal Company, with all the privileges, and subject to all the restrictions, of an act regulating railroad companies, approved the nineteenth day of February, one thousand eight hundred and forty-nine, and the supplements thereto, so far as is consistent with the provisions of this act: *Provided*, That no bid shall be accepted unless the bidder, or the company to whom he shall assign his said bid, shall, on the day of the sale, have deposited in the hands of the governor, or some person duly authorized by him to receive it, the sum of one hundred thousand dollars in cash or State bonds, which shall be forfeited to the use of the Commonwealth if the terms of sale are not complied with; and if the party to whom the same shall be struck down shall not comply with the said conditions, by the payment of one hundred thousand dollars as aforesaid, then it shall be the duty of the governor, if deemed proper by him, to tender the same to the next highest bidder who shall comply with the said conditions: *Provided*, That said next bid is not less than seven millions five hundred thousand dollars, or again expose the said main line to sale, as provided for by the first section of this act: *And provided further*, That if the Pennsylvania Railroad Company shall become the purchasers of said main line at said public sale, or by assignment, as aforesaid, they shall pay, in addition to the purchase money at which it may be struck down, and which shall not be less than the sum of seven and a half millions of dollars, the sum of one and half millions of dollars, the whole amount of sale to be paid in the bonds of the company, bearing interest at the rate of five per centum per annum, payable semi-annually on the thirty-first day of January and July of each year, and which bonds, without further record, shall remain a lien upon the said main line; one hundred thousand dollars of which said bonds shall fall due on the thirty-first day of July, one thousand eight hundred and fifty-eight, and one hundred thousand dollars thereof annually thereafter until the thirty-first day of July, one thousand eight hundred and ninety, when one million of the residue shall fall due, and one million annually thereafter until the whole is paid; and upon the execution and delivery of said bonds to the Treasurer of the State, the Pennsylvania Railroad Company, and the Harrisburg, Portsmouth, Mount Joy and Lancaster Railroad Company, shall, in consideration thereof, be discharged by the Commonwealth forever from the payment of all taxes upon tonnage or freight carried over said railroads; and the said Pennsylvania Railroad Company shall also be released from the payment of all other taxes or duties on its capital stock, bonds, dividends or property, except for school, city, county, borough or township purposes; and

Subject to

Proviso.

$100,000 to be deposited on day of sale, to be forfeited if condition of sale not complied with.

Proviso.

Purchase by Pennsylvania Railroad Company regulated.

When tonnage tax to cease.

Liability for other than State taxes.

May purchase or lease Harrisburg and Lancaster Railroad. that it shall be lawful for the purchasers, or their assigns, either to purchase or lease, hold and use the railroad of the Harrisburg, Portsmouth, Mount Joy and Lancaster Railroad Company, and to straighten and improve the said Philadelphia and Columbia Railroad, and to extend the same to the Delaware river, in the city of Philadelphia; and it shall be further lawful for them to alter, enlarge, and deepen the canal portion of said main line, and to make such additional locks and dams, and to make, in whole or in part, a slack-water navigation as may be deemed expedient; and in the event of a sale or lease as aforesaid by the Harrisburg, Portsmouth, Mount Joy and Lancaster Railroad Company, the said company shall have the power to sell or lease, and the said purchasers, or their assigns, to buy or take on lease said road, and to make and receive respectively all such contracts, deeds or assurances, as may be requisite to carry the same into effect: *Provided*, That the right of the Commonwealth to enter upon, resume and purchase the road of the Pennsylvania Railroad Company, as provided in their charter, shall thereafter cease and determine: *And provided further*, That in case of the refusal of any stockholder or stockholders of said company to comply with the provisions of this act, after the same may have been accepted by a majority of the stockholders of the company, it shall be lawful for said company to pay the stockholder or stockholders so refusing, the full market value of his, her, or their share or shares of stock, and such share or shares shall inure to the benefit of the company, to be disposed of by the directors for the benefit of the balance of the stockholders.

May enlarge and repair works.

Proviso.

Proviso.

SECTION 4. That if the said main line of public works shall be sold to other parties than the Pennsylvania Railroad Company, the purchaser or purchasers shall be entitled to a like credit upon the amount of said purchase money, and for the performance of the conditions of said sale, in behalf of the purchaser, and for the security of the purchase money to the commonwealth, the said purchase money until paid, shall remain a lien on said works; and the individuals or company purchasing as aforesaid, shall, within sixty days after said sale, give a mortgage on the said main line of the public works, and bonds for the amount of the purchase money, and in addition thereto, shall deliver, within ten days after said sale, to the Governor, for the use of the Commonwealth, bonds of the State of Pennsylvania, or of the City of Philadelphia, to the amount of one hundred thousand dollars, and within sixty days the additional amount of one million nine hundred thousand dollars, or in lieu thereof, a like amount of first mortgage bonds of the Penn-

Credit to purchasers.

Purchase money to be a lien.

How to be paid.

sylvania Railroad Company, and payment of the principal of such purchase money shall be made in certificates of loan of the Commonwealth of Pennsylvania, at par or in cash, and of the interest in cash semi-annually on the thirty-first days of July and January in each and every year upon any balance remaining due. Interest, how paid.

SECTION 5. That immediately after the said purchaser or purchasers, or their assigns, shall take possession of the same, the said purchaser or purchasers, or assigns, shall be bound ever thereafter, to keep up in good repair and operating condition, the line of said railroad and canal extending from Hollidaysburg to Philadelphia and so much of the western division as lies between Blairsville and Pittsburgh, until the North-Western Railroad shall be open for business from Blairsville to the Allegheny River; with the necessary toll-houses, water-stations, locks, buildings and other appurtenances; and the said railroad and canal shall be and remain forever a public highway, and the said purchaser or purchasers of the same shall furnish stationary and locomotive engines and motive power, for the use of all persons or companies engaged or wishing to engage in the transportation of tonnage and passengers, at such times and in such manner as not to impair the use and enjoyment of said railroads by such parties, they paying just and fair charges, which shall not exceed the rates of toll on the railroad prescribed in the charter of the Pennsylvania Railroad; and the rates of toll charged upon the canal shall not be more than eighty per centum of those prescribed in the charter of the Union Canal Company, it being the true intent and meaning of this act, that the said sections of canal and railroad and every part thereof, except as is hereinbefore provided, shall be and remain a public highway, and kept open and in repair by the purchaser or purchasers thereof, or assigns as such, for the use and enjoyment of all parties desiring to use and enjoy the same: *Provided*, That said purchasers be authorized to grant, sell and convey, or to lease for a term of years, upon such conditions as may be agreed upon, any part or portion of said canals, and any corporation or association of individuals authorized by this act to purchase the whole, may purchase or lease such portions and hold the same, subject to the conditions and entitled to all the privileges contained in this act: *Provided*, That if the said purchaser or purchasers or their assigns shall decide to abandon the western division, or any part thereof, then they shall be required to lease the same to any party or parties who may desire to keep it open, the expense of keeping up the same devolving entirely upon the lessees, and the purchasers or their assigns being forever exempt from any

Works to be kept in good repair.

And all parties entitled to their uses.

Tolls.

Proviso, That purchasers may sell or lease any part of canals.

Proviso.

5

liability for keeping in navigable condition said western division: *Provided further*, That if the said purchaser or purchasers, or their assigns, shall decide to abandon the Western division or any part thereof, the said purchaser or purchasers, or their assigns, shall within not less than sixty days before such abandonment, purchase from the owner or owners, all the boats then in boating order on the said western division, and all the cars and trucks then in running order on the Allegheny Portage Railroad, at a fair price and valuation, to be agreed upon by the parties; and whenever the said purchaser or purchasers, or their assigns, and any of the said owners cannot agree upon the price and value of any of the said boats, cars or trucks, the parties so failing to agree, shall each select one competent person, and they shall jointly select a third person, or failing to agree in the choice of such third person, the two chosen as aforesaid shall select a third person, and the three persons so chosen shall value and appraise the property, the price whereof could not be agreed upon as aforesaid, and their award shall be binding upon the parties.

Proviso. Abandonment regulated.

Purchases to be made from transporters.

SECTION 6. That the said purchasers may at any time before the maturity of said bonds, and after giving to the commissioners of the sinking fund at least ninety days' notice of their intention so to do, pay off and satisfy the principal of said bonds or of any one or more of them with interest until so paid, at the prescribed rate, and shall then be entitled to receive back or be relieved from a proportionate amount of additional security hereinbefore provided for; and if at any time any one or more of said bonds or the interest due on the same, be and remain unpaid for the space of ninety days from and after the maturity thereof, and the falling due of such interest, then and in that case the Commonwealth shall have full power to re-enter upon and take possession of the property so transferred; and if the Legislature shall not be in session at the time of such default, the Governor shall have full power to appoint one or more persons to take possession thereof in the name of the Commonwealth, and all payments made, and the certificates of State loans as aforesaid deposited with the State Treasurer, shall upon re-entry as aforesaid, be forfeited to the Commonwealth, and the governor shall sue out the mortgage, if any be taken, against any other works of the purchasing company, by *scire facias* in the Supreme Court wherever sitting, under which all the mortgaged works shall be sold, with the rights and franchises of the company, and conveyed to the purchasers by the Treasurer of the Commonwealth, without charge

Bonds may be paid before maturity.

Penalty for non-payment when due.

Sale of works by State for non-payment of purchase money.

for poundage, subject to any liens thereon at the time when mortgaged, which shall remain unaffected thereby.

SECTION 7. That as soon as the purchasers shall have made the payments and delivered the bonds in number, and for amounts equal to and falling due at the time provided for the payment of the respective instalments, and shall have fully complied with the conditions of this act, then the Secretary of the Commonwealth shall transfer, under the great seal of the State, to such purchasers, their successors or assigns, upon such terms and conditions as are mentioned in this act, the whole main line of public works between Philadelphia and Pittsburgh, consisting of the Philadelphia and Columbia Railroad, the Allegheny Portage Railroad, including the new road to avoid the inclined planes, with the necessary and convenient width for the proper use of said railroads, the Eastern Division of the Pennsylvania Canal from Columbia to the Junction, the Juniata Division of the Pennsylvania Canal from the Junction to the eastern terminus of the Allegheny Portage Railroad, and the Western Division of the Pennsylvania Canal from the western terminus of the Allegheny Portage Railroad to Pittsburgh; and including also the right, title and interest of the Commonwealth in the bridge over the Susquehanna at Duncan's Island, together with the same interest in the surplus water power of said canals, with the right to purchase and hold such lands as may be necessary to make the same available, and all the reservoirs, machinery, locomotives, cars, trucks, stationary engines, workshops, tools, water stations, toll houses, offices, stock and materials whatsoever and wheresoever thereunto belonging or held for the use of the same, and together with all the right, title, interest, claim and demands of the Commonwealth of Pennsylvania to all property, real, personal and mixed, belonging to or used in connection with the same by the Commonwealth: *Provided*, That the purchasers of said main line shall take the same and its appurtenances, subject to all contracts and arrangements heretofore made by act of Assembly or otherwise, for and in respect to the use of such works, and shall carry out the same with all persons interested therein, in the same manner as the Commonwealth or its agents are now required to do by law.

Deed to be made by Secretary of Commonwealth.

Proviso.

Purchaser to be subject to all contracts made by State.

SECTION 8. That as soon as the purchasers shall have given notice to the governor of their readiness to take possession of said works, he shall cause notice thereof to be given to all superintendents, toll collectors, officers, and agents of the Commonwealth, employed on or about said railroads and canals, who shall continue nevertheless to discharge the duties of their said offices or employments, (at

Governor to give notice.

Collectors, &c., to continue to act.

Bonds extended. the expense of the purchasers of said main line,) until removed or re-appointed; and the official bonds of said officers or agents shall inure to the use of said purchasers, as to all moneys received or acts done by them on account of said works, subsequent to the time when said purchasers shall take possession as aforesaid.

Purchasers may enter on lands, &c.

SECTION 9. That it shall be lawful for said purchasers, their successors and assigns, and their officers, engineers, contractors and agents, to enter upon any lands adjoining or in the neighborhood of the works, and dig, take and carry away therefrom, any materials necessary for the enlarging, making, altering, deepening or improving said works, or any portion thereof, or for constructing any railroad, canal, bridge, viaduct, dam or other mechanical structure which may be required for the said works, or for making a slackwater navigation, or for improving any works already made: *Provided*, That compensation shall be made or secured to the owner or owners of any such lands or materials as shall be agreed upon between the parties; or if the said purchasers cannot agree with the owner or owners of such lands or materials, then the value of the same shall be ascertained, according to the provisions of the fourth section of the act entitled "A further supplement to an act to incorporate the Pennsylvania Railroad Company," approved the twenty-seventh of March, one thousand eight hundred and forty-eight.

Proviso. Compensation.

Powers of purchasers.

SECTION 10. That said purchasers, their successors and assigns, shall have power and authority to own and employ locomotive engines, cars, boats and horses, and to convey passengers, and freight of whatsoever description, within reasonable time after possession is taken of said works, or any portion thereof, and charge and receive tolls and fare for the passage and transportation of persons and freight; and said purchasers, their successors and assigns, shall have exclusive right to furnish all the motive power on said railroads: *Provided*, That all persons with cars, horses, boats and freight may pass over said works, they paying tolls therefor; and the use of said works shall be governed by such general rules and regulations as said purchasers may from time to time ordain, establish and publish, but no person shall, without the consent of such purchasers, be permitted to use horses, or other animal power on said railroads, or steam on said canals: *And provided*, That no discrimination in tolls or charges, or in priority in passage through the locks, shall ever be made against any boats or tonnage passing to and from the Susquehanna division of the Pennsylvania Canal: *Provided also*, That the rate of toll on freight or tonnage passing over the

Proviso.

Proviso. Tolls.

Proviso.

said canal from the junction to Columbia, coming from the north and West Branch and Susquehanna canals, shall not at any time be greater than the toll now charged on the said canals, as per toll sheet heretofore published by the canal commissioners for the year one thousand eight hundred and fifty-seven: *And provided further*, That the purchasers of the said main line shall at all times keep open the present connection at Columbia and Middletown with the Susquehanna and Tide Water and Union canals, and shall at no time discriminate against the trade or tonnage passing to or from the said canals; neither shall they at any time charge more for boats or other crafts passing the outlet locks at Columbia and Middletown, than is now charged for the passage of boats or similar craft through other outlet locks owned by this Commonwealth.

Proviso. Canal to be kept open.

SECTION 11. That should any company already incorporated by this Commonwealth become the purchaser of said main line, they shall possess, hold and use the same under the provisions of their act of incorporation, and any supplements thereto, modified, however, so as to embrace all the privileges, restrictions and conditions granted by this act in addition thereto; and all provisions in said original act, and any supplements inconsistent with the privileges herein granted shall be and the same are hereby repealed.

Privileges of purchasers being a company incorporated by this Commonwealth.

SECTION 12. That the entire proceeds of the sale of said main line shall be paid to the sinking fund, and applied to the payment of the State debt, according to the provisions of the act entitled "An Act to provide for a sinking fund, and to provide for the gradual and certain extinguishment of the debt of the Commonwealth," approved April tenth, one thousand eight hundred and forty-nine."

Proceeds of sale to be paid into sinking fund.

SECTION 13. That should it be ascertained at any time before the payment of the last instalment provided for, that further legislation is required for passing to the purchasers, their successors and assigns, all the title and interests of this Commonwealth to the said main line, or any portion thereof, or of the property connected therewith or used thereon, then the faith of the Commonwealth of Pennsylvania is hereby pledged for the enactment of all laws and the performance of all acts necessary to carry out the true intent and meaning of this act.

Further legislation to be had if required.

SECTION 14. That all necessary expenses incurred by the governor under the provisions of this act, shall be paid out of any moneys in the treasury not otherwise appropriated, upon warrants drawn by him.

Expenses, how to be paid.

SECTION 15. That the purchaser of said works shall have a perpetual corporate succession; and if the said purchaser shall at any

Privileges may be resumed.

time misuse or abuse any of the privileges granted by this act, the Legislature may revoke all and singular the rights and privileges granted to said company, on a judicial decree of said misuse or abuse being first had and obtained, and thereupon may take for public use the road or roads, canal or canals, so purchased or constructed in pursuance of this act: *Provided*, That in resuming said franchises, no injury shall be done to the corporators of said company; and in taking such road or roads, canal or canals, for public use, full compensation shall be made to the stockholders.

Proviso.

Expenditures by the State to cease on sale of line.

SECTION 16. That in the event of a sale and delivery of said main line as aforesaid, all further payments on account of the appropriations for motive power or other expenses on said main line, as provided in an act to provide for the ordinary expenses of government, the repairs of public canals and railroads, and other general and special appropriations for the year one thousand eight hundred and fifty-seven, shall be supended.

Approved May 16th, 1857.

AN ACT

AUTHORIZING THE PENNSYLVANIA RAILROAD COMPANY TO HOLD REAL ESTATE IN LANCASTER COUNTY.

Company authorized to purchase and hold lands in Lancaster county not exceeding five acres.

SECTION 1. That the Pennsylvania Railroad Company be and is hereby authorized and empowered to purchase and hold lands not exceeding five acres, in the county of Lancaster.

Approved May 16th, 1857.

AN ACT

TO AUTHORIZE THE PENNSYLVANIA RAILROAD COMPANY TO SUBSCRIBE TO THE CAPITAL STOCK OR ENDORSE THE BONDS OF THE CHARTIERS VALLEY RAILROAD COMPANY.

Company authorized to subscribe to capital stock of Chartiers Railroad Company, or

SECTION 1. That the Pennsylvania Railroad Company be authorized to subscribe to the capital stock of the Chartiers Valley Railroad Company, or guarantee the payment of principal and interest upon the mortgage bonds of said Chartiers Valley Railroad Company to an amount not exceeding five hundred thousand dollars, on such terms and conditions as may be agreed upon between the said companies: *Provided*, That the subscription so made shall not be exempt from taxation by virtue of any provisions contained in the act approved May sixteenth, one thousand eight hundred and fifty-seven, for the sale of the main line of the public works. guarantee payment of principal and interest of mortgage bonds of said Company, not exceeding $500.000. Proviso.

Approved May 20th, 1857.

AN ACT

TO AUTHORIZE THE PENNSYLVANIA RAILROAD COMPANY TO SUBSCRIBE TO THE CAPITAL STOCK OF THE HEMPFIELD RAILROAD.

SECTION 1. That the Pennsylvania Railroad Company be authorized to subscribe to the capital stock of the Hempfield Railroad Company, any sum not exceeding one million, on such terms and conditions as may be agreed on between said companies: *And provided*, That this act shall not be of valid effect until accepted by the stockholders of the Pennsylvania Railroad Company, at a meeting to be called for that purpose, as provided in like cases by the charter of the said Company: *Provided, further*, That the stock subscribed in pursuance of this act shall not be relieved from taxation, by virtue of any provisions contained in the bill passed at the present session of the Legislature for the sale of the main line of the public works. Company may subscribe to stock of Hempfield Railroad Company, not exceeding $1.000,000. Proviso. Proviso.

Approved May 20th, 1857.

A SUPPLEMENT

TO THE ACT REGULATING RAILROADS.

SECTION 1. That no lateral or private railroad leading from any ore mine, coal mine, or limestone or other quarry, now having the right to cross, at grade, the track of any railroad authorized to be built by any special charter granted by this Commonwealth, shall Lateral or private railroads from ore mines, &c., not to cros any railroad chartered by this State at more than two crossings, or with more than a double track.

be permitted to cross such track of such chartered railroad at more than two crossings, or with more than a double track; and the proprietors of any such lateral or private railroad leading from any single mine, opening or tunnel, shall, at the point of crossing such chartered railroad, be confined to a double track; and the company owning such chartered railroad shall have the right, in any case, to enforce compliance with the provisions of this section, by refusing to permit more than a double crossing as aforesaid.

Approved May 20th, 1857.

AN ACT

TO AUTHORIZE THE APPOINTMENT OF APPRAISERS TO ASSESS AND REPORT THE DAMAGES SUSTAINED BY TRANSPORTERS AND OTHERS BY REASON OF THE SALE OF THE MAIN LINE OF THE PENNSYLVANIA CANAL.

The Governor to appoint one person and the Pennsylvania Railroad Co. one, and they to appoint a third, to assess damages sustained by the individual transporters on the main line, by reason of the sale of said line.

SECTION 1. That immediately after the passage of this act, the governor be and is hereby authorized and directed to appoint one person who is disinterested, and the Pennsylvania Railroad Company shall appoint another, who shall not be an employee or stockholder of said company, and the persons thus selected shall appoint a third, whose duty shall be to ascertain, appraise, and assess the damages sustained, if any, by the individual transporters on the main line of the public works, or any part thereof, from and after the passage of an act, entitled "An Act for the security of certain transporters on the public works of this Commonwealth," approved the eleventh day of February, one thousand eight hundred and fifty-six, by reason of the sale of the main line: *Provided*, however, that said Pennsylvania Railroad Company shall have notice of the time and place of appointing said appraisers, by service on the President or Vice-President of said corporation for five days; and if said corporation then should neglect or refuse to appoint an appraiser, in that case the governor shall appoint a second person, which two shall select a third.

Provided the Pennsylvania Railroad Company to have 5 days' notice of time and place of appointing appraisers.

If the Company neglects to appoint, the Gov. to appoint the second person, and the two to appoint the third.

Duty of the appraisers.

SECTION 2. That it shall be the duty of the said appraisers immediately after their appointment, after having been severally duly sworn or affirmed, to ascertain and assess the amount of damages sustained by the aforesaid individual transporters by reason of the sale of said main line, under the provisions of the above mentioned act, and report the same, by schedule, designating the different kinds of property upon which damages are assessed, with the value attached to each particular kind, such transporters by name and the amount of damages awarded them during the present session of the Legislature.

SECTION 3. That the said appraisers shall receive for their services, each at the rate of four dollars per day for each and every day they shall be necessarily employed; and the governor is hereby authorized and directed to draw his warrant on the State treasurer for the amount, *Provided*, the time of such examination shall not exceed ten days. Compensation of appraisers.

SECTION 4. That the said appraisers be and they are hereby authorized and empowered to administer oaths and affirmations to witnesses in the investigation hereinbefore provided for. Appraisers to administer oaths and affirmations to witnesses.

Approved March 19th, 1858.

AN ACT

TO AUTHORIZE THE PENNSYLVANIA RAILROAD COMPANY TO MAKE SALES OF CERTAIN REAL ESTATE.

SECTION 1. That hereafter the Pennsylvania Railroad Company shall have full power and authority to make sale of such real estate situated at Powelton, in the city of Philadelphia, or elsewhere, as the said company may at any time hold, or be in any way interested in or entitled to, and which in the opinion of the directors of the said company shall not be necessary for the uses and purposes of said company, and to assure to the purchasers of the same, by good and effectual title, the premises which shall be sold under the authority of this act: *Provided, however*, That the authority herein contained, shall not be so construed or exercised as to discharge any lien that the Commonwealth of Pennsylvania may have on any of the real estate sold and conveyed in pursuance of this act. Company to have power to sell and convey such of its real estate as in the opinion of the directors is not necessary for the uses and purposes of the company. (See ante, pp. 53, 58.) Provided the authority herein given shall not discharge any lien the commonwealth may have on such real estate.

Approved April 1st, 1858.

AN ACT

ANNEXING THE COUNTY OF SCHUYLKILL TO THE EASTERN DISTRICT OF THE SUPREME COURT, AND FOR OTHER PURPOSES.

Councils authorized to regulate tolls on city railroads. Proviso.

SECTION 3. That the Select and Common Councils of the City of Philadelphia be and they are hereby authorized and empowered to pass ordinances to require the owners or agents of cars traveling on the railroads in Broad, High, Third, and Dock streets, in the city of Philadelphia, to deliver a certificate of the contents of each car, and the number of passengers contained therein, and of the distance they have been conveyed on said railroads, and to require the owners or agents of such cars to pay toll for the same: *Provided*, That the toll charged shall be the same toll as may be charged on the Pennsylvania railroad, [and that all distances under half a mile shall be charged as half a mile, and all distances over half a mile and under one mile, shall be charged as one mile.]*

Power of mayor, &c., when ordinances are violated.

SECTION 4. That it shall be lawful for the mayor, aldermen and citizens of Philadelphia to provide for the punishment of any person or persons who shall refuse or omit to comply with the provisions of the ordinances which may be enacted by virtue of this act, by imposing a fine, to be recovered in the same manner as penalties for the violation of the ordinances of the City of Philadelphia are now by law recoverable.

Approved August 2d, 1842.

AN ACT

RELATIVE TO THE OBSTRUCTING OF THE CROSSINGS OF PUBLIC ROADS BY LOCOMOTIVES AND CARS.

Penalty for obstructing the crossings of public streets, with locomotives or cars.

SECTION 1. That it shall not be lawful for any railroad company to block up the passage of any crossings of public streets or roads, or obstruct the said crossings with their locomotives or cars; and if any engineer or other agent of any such railroad company, shall

---

* Repealed by act of May 13th, 1856, section 41, ante, page 60.

obstruct or block up such crossings, he or they shall be subject to a penalty of twenty-five dollars, to be recovered, with costs, in the name of the Commonwealth of Pennsylvania, before a justice of the peace, one-half of such penalty shall be paid to the informer or informers, and the remaining half shall be paid into the treasury of the Commonwealth: *Provided*, That in the event of the said engineer or agent being unable to pay the said penalty, then, and in that case, the said railroad company employing the said engineer or agent, shall pay the penalty aforesaid.

Proviso. If engineer be unable to pay, then the company is liable.

Approved March 20th, 1845.

PENNSYLVANIA

GENERAL RAILROAD ACT.

AN ACT

REGULATING RAILROAD COMPANIES.

SECTION 1. That whenever a special act of the general assembly shall hereafter be passed, authorizing the incorporation of a company for the construction of a railroad within this commonwealth, the commissioners named in such act, or any five of them, shall have power to open books for receiving subscriptions to the capital stock of such company, at such time or times, and at such place or places as they may deem expedient, after having given at least twenty days' notice, in one or more newspapers, published in the county where books of subscription are to be opened; and at the times and places so designated and named in the public notices to be given, as aforesaid, the said commissioners, or any two of them, shall attend and furnish to all persons duly qualified, who shall offer to subscribe, an opportunity of so doing; and it shall be lawful for all such persons, and for all firms and copartnerships, by themselves or by persons duly authorized, to subscribe for shares in said stock; and the said books shall be kept open at least six hours in every day, for the term of three juridical days, or until there shall have been subscribed the whole number of shares authorized by the special act; and if at the expiration of three days, the books aforesaid shall not have the number of shares therein subscribed, the said commissioners may adjourn, from time to time, and to such places as they may deem proper, until the whole number of shares authorized, as aforesaid, shall be subscribed, of which adjournment the commissioners aforesaid shall give such public notice as the occasion may require; and when the whole number of shares shall be subscribed the books shall be closed: *Provided always*, That no subscription for such stock shall be valid unless the party or parties making the same shall, at the time of subscribing, pay to the said commissioners five dollars on each and every share subscribed, for the use of the company.

Commissioners.

Subscriptions.

Who may subscribe.

Proviso.

SECTION 2. That when ten per centum on the capital stock, as provided by any special act of incorporation, shall have been subscribed, and five dollars paid on each and every share, as aforesaid, the said commissioners, or such of them as shall have acted, shall certify to the governor, under their hands and seals, the names of the subscribers, and the number of shares subscribed by each, and that five dollars on each share have been paid, whereupon the gov-

Letters patent. ernor shall, by letters patent, under his hand and seal of the commonwealth, create and constitute the subscribers, and if the subscription be not full at the time, those who shall thereafter subscribe to the number of shares aforesaid, their successors and assigns, into Incorporate. a body politic and corporate, in deed and in law, by the name, style Style. and title designated by the special act of assembly; and by the said name, style and title, the said subscribers shall have perpetual suc- Privileges. cession, with all the privileges, franchises and immunities incident to a corporation, and be able to sue and be sued, plead and be impleaded, in all courts of record and elsewhere, and to purchase, receive, have, hold, use and enjoy to them and their successors, goods, chattels and estate, real and personal, of what kind and nature soever, and the same from time to time to sell, exchange, mortgage, grant, alien or otherwise dispose of, and to make dividends of such portion of the profits as they may deem proper; and also to make and have a common seal, and the same to alter and renew at pleas- By-laws. ure, and also to ordain, establish and put in execution, such by-laws, ordinances and regulations as shall appear necessary or convenient for the government of said corporation, not being contrary to the constitution and laws of the United States, or of this commonwealth, and generally to do all and singular the matters and things which to them it shall lawfully appertain to do for the well being of said corporation, and the due ordering and management of the affairs there- Proviso. of: *Provided*, That nothing herein contained shall be construed as in any way giving to such corporation any banking privileges whatever, or any other liberties, privileges or franchises but such as may be necessary or convenient to the procuring, owning, making, maintaining, regulating and using their railroad, the locomotives, machinery, cars and other appendages thereof, and the conveyance of passengers, the transportation of goods, merchandise and other Proviso. commodities thereon: *And provided further*, That such company shall not purchase or hold any real estate, except such as may be necessary or convenient for the making or constructing of their railroad, or for the furnishing of materials therefor, and for the accommodation of depots, offices, warehouses, machine shops, toll houses, engine and water stations, and other appropriate appurtenances, and for the persons and things employed or used in and about the same.

SECTION 3. That the commissioners named as aforesaid, or such of them as shall have acted, shall, as soon as conveniently may be after the said letters patent shall be obtained, appoint a time and Organization. place for the subscribers to meet to organize the company, and shall give at least two weeks' notice thereof in the manner provided for in the first section of this act; and the said subscribers, when met, shall elect, by a majority of the votes present, to be given in person or by proxy, a president and twelve directors, the president and a majority of whom shall be resident citizens of this commonwealth, and shall be owners respectively of at least three shares in the stock of such company; and the said president and directors shall conduct and manage the affairs and business of said company, until the second Monday in January then next ensuing, and until others are chosen; and may make, ordain and establish such by-laws, rules, orders and regulations, and perform such other matters and things as are by this act authorized: *Provided*, that in case of the resignation, death or removal of the president, the directors shall, by a majority of votes, supply the vacancy until the next annual election. Officers. Proviso.

SECTION 4. That the stockholders of such company shall meet on the second Monday in January in every year, at such place as may be fixed on by the by-laws, of which notice shall be given at least two weeks previously by the secretary, in the manner before mentioned, and choose, by a majority of the votes present, a president and twelve directors, qualified as aforesaid, for the ensuing year, who shall continue in office until the next annual election, and until others are chosen; at which annual meeting the said stockholders shall have full power and authority to make, alter or repeal, by a majority of votes given, any or all such by-laws, rules, orders and regulations as aforesaid, and do and perform every other corporate act authorized by their charter: the stockholders may meet at such other times and places as they may be summoned by the president and directors, in such manner and form, and giving such notice as may be prescribed by the by-laws; and the president, on the request in writing of any number of stockholders representing not less than one tenth in interest, shall call a special meeting, giving the like notice, and stating specifically the objects of the meeting; and the objects special in such notice, and no other, shall be acted on at such special meeting. Annual meeting. Special meeting

SECTION 5. The elections for directors provided for in this act, shall be conducted as follows, to wit: at the first election the commissioners shall appoint three stockholders to be judges of the said election, and to hold the same; and at every succeeding election the directors for the time being, shall appoint three stockholders for the like purpose; and the persons so appointed by said commissioners and directors shall not be eligible to an election as a director at said election, and shall respectively take and subscribe Elections, how conducted.

an oath or affirmation, before an alderman or justice of the peace, well and truly and according to law, to conduct such election to the best of their knowledge and ability; and the said judges shall decide upon the qualifications of voters, and when the election is closed, shall count the votes and declare who have been elected; and if at any time it shall happen that an election of directors shall not be made at the time specified, the corporation shall not for that reason be dissolved; but it shall be lawful to hold and make such election of directors on any day within three months thereafter, by giving at least ten days' previous notice of the time and place of holding said election in the manner aforesaid; and the directors of the preceding year shall, in that case, continue in office, and be invested with all powers belonging to them as such, until others are elected in their stead. In case of the death or resignation of a director, or a failure to elect in case of a tie vote, the vacancy may be filled by the board of directors; at all general meetings or elections by the stockholders, each share of stock shall entitle the holder thereof to one vote, and each ballot shall have endorsed thereon the number of shares thereby represented; but no share or shares transferred within sixty days next preceding any election or general meeting of the stockholders, shall entitle the holder or holders thereof to vote at any such election or general meeting; nor shall any proxy be received, or entitle the holder to vote, unless the same shall bear date, and have been duly executed within the three months next preceding such election or general meeting.

Powers.

SECTION 6. That the president and directors of such company, for the time being, are hereby authorized and empowered to exercise all the powers granted to the corporation; they shall meet at such times and places as shall be by them deemed most convenient for the transaction of their business, and when met, seven shall be a quorum to do business; the president, if present, shall preside at all meetings of the board, and when absent the board shall appoint a president pro tem.; they shall keep minutes of their proceedings, fairly entered in a suitable book to be kept for that purpose; they shall choose a secretary and treasurer, and may appoint or employ all such officers, engineers, agents, superintendents, artisans, workmen, or other persons, as in their opinions may be necessary or proper in the management of the affairs and business of said corporation, at such times, in such manner, and under such regulations as they may from time to time determine; they shall fix the amount of the salaries and wages of such officers and persons employed by

Quorum.

them, and they may require bond, with security, in such amounts as they may deem necessary, of each or any of said officers or other persons by them appointed or employed, for the faithful discharge of their duties, and generally to do all such other acts, matters and things as by this act and the by-laws and regulations of the said company they may be authorized to do.

SECTION 7. That the president and directors of such company first chosen, shall procure certificates or evidences of stock for all the shares of such company, and shall deliver one or more certificates or evidences, signed by the president, countersigned by the treasurer, and sealed with the common seal of the corporation, to each person or party entitled to receive the same, according to the number of shares by him, her or them respectively subscribed or held, which certificates or evidences of stock shall be transferable at the pleasure of the holder, in a suitable book or books to be kept by the company for that purpose, in person or by attorney duly authorized, in the presence of the president or treasurer, subject, however, to all payments due or to become due thereon; and the assignee or party to whom the same shall have been so transferred, shall thereupon be a member of said corporation, and have and enjoy all the immunities, privileges and franchises, and be subject to all the liabilities, conditions and penalties incident thereto, in the same manner as the original subscriber would have been: *Provided*, That no certificate shall be transferred so long as the holder thereof is indebted to said company, unless the board of directors shall consent thereto: *And provided*, That no such transfer of stock shall have the effect of discharging any liabilities or penalties theretofore incurred by the owner thereof.

Certificates of stock. Transferable. Proviso.

SECTION 8. The capital stock of such company shall be divided into shares of fifty dollars each, and shall be called in and paid at such times and places, and in such proportions and instalments, not, however, exceeding five dollars per share in any period of thirty days, as the directors shall require, of which public notice shall be given for at least two weeks next preceding the time or times appointed for that purpose, in the manner above mentioned; and if any stockholder shall neglect to pay such proportion or instalment so called for at the time and place appointed, he, she or they shall be liable to pay, in addition to the proportion or instalment so called for, at the rate of one per cent. per month for the delay of such payment; and if the same and the additional penalty, or any part thereof, shall remain unpaid for the period of six months, he,

Capital stock. Shares. Instalments.

Forfeiture. she or they shall, at the discretion of the directors, forfeit to the use of the company all right, title and interest in and to every and all share or shares, on account of which such default in payment may be made as aforesaid, or the directors may, at their option, cause suit to be brought before any competent tribunal, for the recovery of the amount due on such shares, together with the penalty of one per cent. per month as aforesaid; and in the event of a forfeiture, the share or shares so forfeited may be disposed of at the discretion of the president and directors, under such rules and regulations as may be prescribed by the by-laws. No stockholder shall be entitled to vote at any election, nor at any general or special meeting of the company, on whose share or shares any instalment or arrearages may be due more than thirty days next preceding said election or meeting; Proviso. *Provided*, That no forfeiture of stock shall release or discharge the owner thereof from any liabilities or penalties incurred prior to the time of such forfeiture.

Dividends. SECTION 9. That the dividends of so much of the profits of such company as shall appear advisable to the directors, shall be declared in the months of July and January in each and every year, and be paid to the stockholders or their legal representatives, on application at the office of such company, at any time after the expiration of ten days from the time of declaring the same; but the said dividends shall in no case exceed the amount of the net profits actually acquired by the company, so that the capital stock shall never be impaired thereby; and if the said directors shall make any dividend which shall impair the capital stock of the company, the directors consenting thereto shall be liable, in their individual capacities, to such company, for the amount of the capital stock so divided, recoverable by action of debt as in other cases; and each director present when such dividend shall be declared, shall be considered as consenting thereto, unless he forthwith enter his protest on the minutes of the board, and give public notice to the stockholders of the declaring of such dividend.

Locate, fix, mark and determine route, &c. SECTION 10. That the president and directors of such company shall have power and authority by themselves, their engineers, superintendents, agents, artizans and workmen, to survey, ascertain, locate, fix, mark and determine, such route for a railroad as they may deem expedient, not, however, passing through any burying ground or place of public worship, or any dwelling house in the occupancy of the owner or owners thereof, without his, her, or their consent, and not, except in the neighborhood of deep cuttings, or high embankments, or places selected for sidelings, turn-outs, depots, engine or water stations, to exceed sixty feet in width, and thereon to lay down, erect, construct and establish a railroad, with one or more tracks, with such branches or lateral roads as may be specially authorized, and with such bridges, viaducts, turn-outs, sidelings, or other devices as they may deem necessary or useful between the points named in the special act incorporating such company, commencing at or within, and extending to or into any town, city or village, named as the place of beginning or terminus of such road; and in like manner, by themselves, or other persons by them appointed or employed as aforesaid, to enter upon and into, and occupy all land on which the said railroad or depots, warehouses, offices, toll houses, engines and water stations, other buildings or appurtenances hereinbefore mentioned may be located, or which may be necessary or convenient for the erection of the same, or for any purpose necessary or useful in the construction, maintenance or repairs of said railroad, and therein and thereon to dig, excavate and embank, make, grade, and lay down and construct the same; and it shall in like manner be lawful for such company, their officers, agents, engineers, contractors or workmen, with their implements and beasts of draught or burden, to enter upon any lands adjoining or in the neighborhood of their railroads so to be constructed, and to quarry, dig, cut, take and carry away therefrom, any stone, gravel, clay, sand, earth, wood, or other suitable material necessary or proper for the construction of any bridges, viaduct or other building, which may be required for the use, maintenance or repairs of said railroad: *Provided*, That before such company shall enter upon or take possession of any such lands or materials, they shall make ample compensation to the owner or owners thereof, or tender adequate security therefor: *Provided further*, That the timber used in the construction or repair of said railroad, shall be obtained from the owner thereof, only by agreement or purchase: *And provided further*, That whenever any company shall locate its road in and upon any street or alley, in any city or borough, ample compensation shall be made to the owners of lots fronting upon such street or alley, for any damages they may sustain, by reason of any excavation or embankment made in the construction of such road, to be ascertained as other damages are authorized to be ascertained by this act.

Proviso.

Proviso.

Proviso.

SECTION 11. That when the said company cannot agree with the owner or owners of any lands or materials, for the compensation proper for the damage done or likely to be done to, or sustained by

Damages, how ascertained and adjusted.

any such owner or owners of such lands or materials, which such company may enter upon, use or take away, in pursuance of the authority hereinbefore given, or by reason of the absence or legal incapacity of any such owner or owners, no such compensation can be agreed upon, the Court of Common Pleas of the proper county, on application thereto by petition, either by said company or owner or owners, or any one in behalf of either, shall appoint seven discreet and disinterested freeholders of said county, neither of whom shall be residents or owners of property upon or adjoining the line of such railroad, and appoint a time, not less than twenty nor more than thirty days thereafter, for said viewers to meet at or upon the premises where the damages are alleged to be sustained, of which time and place ten days' notice shall be given by the petitioner to the said viewers and the other party; and the said viewers or any five of them, having been first duly sworn or affirmed, faithfully, justly and impartially to decide, and true report to make concerning all matters and things to be submitted to them, and in relation to which they are authorized to inquire in pursuance of the provisions of this act, and having viewed the premises, they shall estimate and determine the quantity, quality and value of said lands so taken or occupied, or to be so taken or occupied, or the materials so used or taken away, as the case may be, and having a due regard to and making just allowance for the advantages which may have resulted, or which may seem likely to result to the owner or owners of said land or materials, in consequence of the making or opening of said railroad, and of the construction of works connected therewith; and after having made a fair and just comparison of said advantages and disadvantages, they shall estimate and determine whether any, and if any, what amount of damages has been or may be sustained, and to whom payable, and make report thereof to the said court; and if any damages be awarded, and the report be confirmed by the said court, judgment shall be entered thereon; and if the amount thereof be not paid within thirty days after the entry of such judgment, execution may then issue thereon as in other cases of debt, for the sum so awarded, and the costs and expenses incurred shall be defrayed by the said railroad company; and each of said viewers shall be entitled to one dollar and fifty cents per day for every day necessarily employed in the performance of the duties herein prescribed, to be paid by such railroad company.

SECTION 12. That whenever, in the construction of such road or roads, it shall be necessary to cross or intersect any established road or way, it shall be the duty of the president and directors of the said company, so to construct the said road across such established road or way, as not to impede the passage or transportation of persons or property along the same; and that, for the accommodation of all persons owning or possessing land through which the said railroad may pass, it shall be the duty of such company to make or cause to be made, a good and sufficient causeway or causeways, whenever the same may be necessary to enable the occupant or occupants of said lands to cross or pass over the same, with wagons, carts and implements of husbandry, as occasion may require; and the said causeway or causeways, when so made, shall be maintained and kept in good repair by such company; and if the said company shall neglect or refuse, on request, to make such causeway or causeways, or when made, to keep the same in good order, the said company shall be liable to pay any person aggrieved thereby, all damages sustained by such person in consequence of such neglect or refusal; such damages to be assessed and ascertained in the same manner as provided in the last section for the assessment of damages: *Provided*, That the said company shall, in no case, be required to make or cause to be made, more than one causeway through each plantation or lot of land, for the accommodation of any one person owning or possessing land through which the said railroad may pass; and where any public road shall cross such railroad, the person owning or possessing land through which the said public road may pass, shall not be entitled to require the company to erect or keep in repair any causeway or bridge for the accommodation of the occupant of said land.

Causeways.

To be kept in good repair, &c.

Proviso.

SECTION 13. That if any such railroad company shall find it necessary to change the site of any portion of any turnpike or public road, they shall cause the same to be so re-constructed forthwith, at their own proper expense, on the most favorable location, and in as perfect a manner as the original road: *Provided*, That the damages incurred in changing the location of any road authorized by this section, shall be ascertained and paid by such company, in the same manner as is provided for in regard to the location and construction of their own road.

Change of location.

Proviso.

SECTION 14. That in all suits or actions against such company, the service of process on the president, secretary, treasurer, engineer, agent, or any director of the same, shall be good and available in law; but no suit or action shall be prosecuted by any person or persons, for any penalties incurred under this act, unless such suit or action shall be commenced within two years next after the offence

Service of process.

committed or cause of action accrued; and the defendants in such suit or action may plead the general issue, and give this act and the special matter in evidence, and that the same was done in pursuance and by authority of this act.

Penalty for committing injuries to works, &c.

SECTION 15. That if any person or persons shall wilfully and knowingly break, injure or destroy any railroad authorized by special act of assembly, or any part thereof, or any edifice, device, property or work, or any part thereof, or any machinery, engine, car, implement or utensil, erected, owned or used by such company, in pursuance of this act, he, she or they so offending shall forfeit and pay to such company three times the actual damage so sustained, to be sued for and recovered with full costs, before any tribunal having cognizance thereof, by action in the name and for the use of the company.

Penalty for misdemeanor.

SECTION 16. That if any person or persons shall willfully and maliciously remove or destroy any part of the road, property, buildings or other works belonging to such company or place, designedly and with evil intent, any obstruction on the line of such railroad, so as to jeopard the safety or endanger the lives of persons traveling on or over the same, such person or persons so offending shall be deemed guilty of a misdemeanor, and shall, on conviction, be imprisoned in the county jail or penitentiary, at the discretion of the court, for a term not more than three years: *Provided*, That nothing herein contained shall prevent the company from pursuing any other appropriate remedy at law in such cases.

Proviso.

SECTION 17. That at each annual meeting of the stockholders of any such company, the president and managers of the preceding year shall exhibit to them a full and complete statement of the affairs and proceedings of the company for such year, with all such matters as shall be necessary to convey to the stockholders a full knowledge of the condition and affairs of said company, and the said president and directors of every such company shall, whenever required, furnish to the legislature, or either branch thereof, a full and authentic report of their affairs and transactions, or such information relating thereto as may be demanded of them.

Statement of affairs, &c.

Public highways.

SECTION 18. That upon the completion of any railroad authorized as aforesaid, the same shall be esteemed a public highway for the conveyance of passengers and the transportation of freight, subject to such rules and regulations, in relation to the same, and to the size and construction of wheels, cars and carriages, the weight of loads, and all other matters and things connected with the use of said railroad as the president and directors may prescribe and direct: *Pro-*

vided, That the said company shall have the exclusive control of the motive power, and may from time to time establish, demand and receive such rates of toll, or other compensation, for the use of such road, and of said motive power, and for the conveyance of passengers, the transportation of merchandise and commodities, and the cars or other vehicles containing the same, or otherwise passing over or on the said railroad, as to the president and directors shall seem reasonable: *Provided, however, nevertheless*, That said rates of toll and motive power charges so to be established, demanded or received, when the cars used for such conveyance or transportation are owned or furnished by others, shall not exceed two and one half cents per mile for each passenger, three cents per mile for each ton of two thousands pounds of freight, three cents per mile for each passenger or baggage car, and two cents per mile for each burden or freight car, every four wheels being computed a car; and in the transportation of passengers no charge shall be made to exceed three cents per mile for through passengers, and three and a half cents per mile for way passengers. Proviso. Proviso. Toll.

SECTION 19. That if any company incorporated as aforesaid, shall not commence the construction of their proposed railroad within three years, and complete and open the same for use, with at least one track, within the term prescribed by the special act authorizing the same, or if, after completion, the said railroad shall be suffered to go into decay, and be impassable for the term of two years, then this charter shall be null and void, except so far as to compel the said company to make reparation for damages. Commencement and completion of road.

SECTION 20. That if any company incorporated as aforesaid shall at any time misuse or abuse any of the privileges granted by this act, or by the special act of incorporation, the legislature may revoke all and singular the rights and privileges so granted to such company; and the legislature hereby reserves the power to resume, alter or amend any charter granted under this act, and take for public use any road constructed in pursuance of such charter: *Provided*, That in resuming, altering or amending said charters, no injustice shall be done to the corporators; and that in taking such roads for public use, full compensation shall be made to the stockholders. Reservation. Proviso.

Approved February 19th, 1849.

ORDINANCES

AFFECTING THE COMPANY.

ORDINANCES

OF THE

CITY OF PHILADELPHIA.

AN ORDINANCE

PROVIDING FOR A SUPERINTENDENT OF THE RAILROAD ALONG HIGH, THIRD AND DOCK STREETS, AND REGULATING THE TRAVELING THEREON, AND FOR THE BETTER REGULATION OF THE TRAVELING UPON THE RAILROAD IN BROAD STREET.

Supplied.

Duties of superintendent.

SECTION 1. [Provided for the appointment of a superintendent of the railroad along High, Third and Dock streets,] whose duty it shall be to receive all tolls (not otherwise provided for) which may be chargeable for traveling on said road, and pay the same weekly into the city treasury; he shall also attend to keeping the said road clean and in good traveling order, attend to any repairs which may be necessary, and perform such other duties as may be enjoined upon him, either by ordinance, or the committee on public highways. [Rest of section supplied.]

Tolls, how to be charged.

SECTION 2. That owners or agents of cars or other vehicles may have the privilege of contracting for traveling on said railroad, and also on the railroad on Broad street, by the quarter, payable in advance to the [city commissioners*]; all tolls to be charged at the same rates as those charged on the Columbia Railroad.

SECTION 3. [Repealed.]

Penalty for obstructing the road.

SECTION 4. That it shall not be lawful for any person or persons to unload any car or other vehicle on said railroad, or drive any cart, wagon or other vehicle, except railroad cars, along said road, or occupy the same, or obstruct in any manner the traveling of cars thereon, or allow any car or cars not in actual service to remain on any part of said road, under the penalty of five dollars for each offence, to be recovered in manner as hereinbefore mentioned.

---

* Chief Commissioner of Highways.

Cars to be registered and numbered.

SECTION 5. That it shall not be lawful for any person or persons to use any car or cars or other vehicles upon said road, or upon the railroad in Broad street, designed or employed for the conveyance of passengers, without having the owners' or agents' names thereof first registered in the office of the city commissioners, and a number assigned to each car or vehicle, and the number so assigned to be legibly affixed on each side of the body of the car or vehicle, under a penalty of five dollars for each offence, to be recovered in manner as hereinbefore mentioned.

Bells to be attached to horses, under a penalty.

SECTION 6. That it shall be the duty of the owners or agents of cars or other vehicles, to have attached to the horses or other animals, while drawing cars upon said road, and also upon the said railroad in Broad street, a suitable bell or bells, under a penalty of five dollars for each offence, to be recovered as hereinbefore mentioned.

Regulating the time of traveling.

SECTION 7. That it shall be the duty of the [city commissioners,] under the direction of the committee on public highways, to regulate the time not otherwise provided for, for traveling the railroad along Third and High streets, from Dock to Eighth street; such regulations shall be published by the president of the Board of city commissioners, in at least two daily papers published in the city of Philadelphia, immediately after they shall have been made, or whenever after they may be altered, and any violation of any such regulation shall subject the offender to a penalty of five dollars for each offence, to be recovered as hereinbefore mentioned.

Passed January 11th, 1838.

A SUPPLEMENT

TO AN ORDINANCE PROVIDING FOR A SUPERINTENDENT OF THE RAILROAD ALONG HIGH, THIRD AND DOCK STREETS, AND REGULATING THE TRAVEL THEREON.

At what rate cars are to be drawn, and by what power.

SECTION 1. That every car or other vehicle used on said road shall be drawn by animal power, at a rate not exceeding a walk, under a penalty of five dollars for each offence; and at no time shall they be drawn or propelled by steam, under a penalty of fifty dollars for each offence; said penalties to be sued for and recovered in the same manner as debts under one hundred dollars are by law recoverable.

Passed March 1st, 1838.

AN ORDINANCE

TO PROVIDE FOR THE COLLECTION OF TOLLS ON MERCHANDISE AND MERCHANDISE CARS, USING THE RAILROAD ON BROAD, HIGH, THIRD AND DOCK STREETS.

SECTION 1. That from and after the first day of November, 1840, all merchandise and merchandise cars shall be charged for the use of the railroad in Broad, High, Third and Dock streets, the same rate of toll as is now charged on the Columbia railroad, the said toll to be collected in such manner as shall be designated by the committee on public highways. Tolls to be collected on city railroad after Nov. 1, 1840. Rate of tolls.

SECTION 2. That the owners or agents of merchandise or merchandise cars may have the privilege of contracting for the use of the said road with the committee on public highways. Owners of cars may contract for use of road.

SECTION 3. That so much of any ordinance as is inconsistent herewith, be and the same is hereby repealed. Repeal.

Passed Sept. 24th, 1840.

AN ORDINANCE

TO PROVIDE FOR THE COLLECTION OF TOLLS ON THE RAILROAD ON BROAD, HIGH, THIRD AND DOCK STREETS, AND TO REGULATE THE TRAVEL THEREON.

SECTION 1. That the owner or owners, agent or agents, of cars traveling on the railroad in Broad, High, Third and Dock streets, shall deliver to the superintendent of the said railroad a certificate of the contents of each car, and the number of passengers conveyed therein, and the distance the same have been conveyed on said railroad; and the said owner or agent shall pay toll for the same, to the said superintendent, for the use of the city, at the same rate as may be arranged at the time on the Pennsylvania railroad, [and all distances under half a mile shall be charged as half a mile, and all distances over half a mile and under one mile, shall be charged as Owners to deliver certificates. Rate of toll.

Proviso. one mile:*] *Provided*, That the owners of cars or merchandise may contract as heretofore for the use of said road.

Penalty. SECTION 2. That if any owner or owners, agent or agents, as aforesaid, shall refuse or neglect to deliver the certificate before mentioned, he, she or they shall forfeit and pay for every such neglect the sum of three dollars, to be recovered in the same manner as penalties for the violation of the ordinances of the city of Philadelphia are now by law recoverable.

Cars to be provided with brakes. SECTION 3. That every car traveling on said railroad shall be provided with a suitable brake, and in default thereof the owner, agent, or person having charge of such car, shall forfeit and pay the sum of three dollars, to be recovered in the manner hereinbefore mentioned.

Passed Nov. 24th, 1842.

AN ORDINANCE

FOR THE CONSTRUCTION OF A RAILROAD FROM THE FOOT OF HIGH STREET, ON THE WEST SIDE OF THE RIVER SCHUYLKILL, TO CONNECT WITH THE RAILROAD ON BROAD STREET.

Construction of railroad in High st., from west side of bridge to Broad st., authorized. SECTION 1. That the committee on city property be authorized and directed to cause to be constructed a railroad to connect with the railroad about to be constructed on the west side of the river Schuylkill, to avoid the inclined plane on the Columbia railroad, and continue the same across the permanent bridge, and along High street, within the city of Philadelphia, eastwardly, until it intersects the railroad in Broad street.

[SECTIONS 2 and 3 temporary.]

Passed August 2d, 1849.

---

* Altered by Act of May 13, 1856, sec. 41, ante, p. 60.

A SUPPLEMENT

TO AN ORDINANCE PASSED THE 24TH DAY OF NOVEMBER, 1842, ENTITLED "AN ORDINANCE TO PROVIDE FOR THE COLLECTION OF TOLLS ON THE RAILROAD IN BROAD, HIGH, THIRD AND DOCK STREETS, AND TO REGULATE TRAVEL THEREON."

Rate of toll to be charged for the use of the railroad west of Broad street.

[Bridge to be computed as one mile.]

SECTION 1. That the same rate of toll shall be charged for the use of the railroad in High street, west of Broad, as is by the ordinance to which this is a supplement charged for the use of railroads therein mentioned, [except that, in the computation of tolls, the railroad on the bridge over the Schuylkill at High street shall be considered as one mile,]* and the provisions in the said ordinance contained, in relation to the duties of the owner or owners, agent or agents, of cars traveling on the railroads therein mentioned, shall be applied to the railroad herein mentioned: *Provided*, That the owners of cars and merchandise may contract for the use of said road.

Owners of cars may contract for use of road.

No car to pass over the bridge without permit.

SECTION 2. That no car shall be permitted to pass on said road, over said bridge, without a permit from the superintendent of the railroad, which permit the said superintendent is hereby required to deliver to the person having charge of such car, whenever the toll for the use of said road by such car shall have been paid.

Penalty for violation thereof.

SECTION 3. That if any car shall pass over said bridge without such permit, the owner or owners, agent or agents, or persons having charge thereof, shall forfeit and pay the sum of five dollars; and if passage over the said bridge is refused for want of said permit, then if the said car shall hinder or obstruct the passage of other cars over the said bridge, or on the said railroad in High street west of Broad, the owner or owners, agent or agents, or person having charge of such car, shall forfeit and pay the sum of five dollars, the said penalties to be sued for and recovered in the manner that penalties for violation of ordinances are by law sued for and recoverable.

Passed January 16*th*, 1851.

* Altered by Act of March 13, 1856, sec. 41, ante, page 60.

AN ORDINANCE

TO PROVIDE FOR THE REGULATION OF TURN-OUTS FROM THE CITY RAILROAD.

Committee on public highways to authorize all turn-outs on city railroads.

SECT. 1. That the committee on public highways be and they are hereby authorized to grant permission to persons or companies owning or occupying property situated upon the street through which the railroads belonging to the city are laid, to attach turn-outs or bolting-tracks thereto, said turn-outs or bolting tracks to be laid in such manner as to conform to the established heighths and levels of the streets in which they may be placed; and such permission shall be in writing and shall be subject to the provisions of this and all other ordinances relating to the railroad in the city of Philadelphia.

To establish regulations.

SECT. 2. That it shall be lawful for the committee on public highways, from time to time, to make, establish and put in force, such rules, regulations and restrictions, in relation to such turn-outs or bolting-tracks, their construction and materials, and the repairing thereof, as to the said committee shall seem fit and proper; and no turn-out, bolting-track, or other fixture shall be attached to the said railroad, or laid over or on any street, or be considered as repaired, unless the same shall conform in every particular to the rules and regulations so adopted.

To be repaired under direction of superintendent of city railroad.

SECT. 3. That all such turn-outs, bolting-tracks or other fixtures, shall be laid or repaired under the direction and inspection of the superintendent of the city railroad; and if any person or persons shall construct, lay down or repair any turn-out, bolting-track or other fixture, contrary to the provisions of this ordinance, or of any regulation adopted by the committee on public highways, the person or persons so offending shall forfeit and pay the sum of twenty dollars, to be sued for and recovered in the manner that penalties for the breach of ordinances are by law recoverable, and in addition thereto, such turn-out, bolting-track or other fixture shall be forthwith removed.

Penalty for neglect to repair.

SECT. 4. That if any turn-out, bolting-track, switch, turning-platform or other fixture, shall be out of order and repair, and the owner or person having charge thereof, shall refuse or neglect to repair or put the same in good order, after five days' notice from the superintendent of the city railroad, the same shall be taken up and removed, under the direction of the committee on public highways, and the owner or person having charge of such turn-out, bolting-track, switch, turning-platform or other fixture, shall also forfeit and pay the sum of twenty dollars, to be sued for and recovered in the manner that penalties for the breach of ordinances are by law recoverable; *Provided*, that the turn-out, bolting-track, switch, turning-platform, or fixture, after being removed, shall not be replaced unless by permission of the committee on public highways, nor until all the expenses of such removal shall first be paid. Proviso.

SECT. 5. That the person or persons to whom permission shall be granted to attach any turn-out, bolting-track, or other fixture to the city railroad, as is herein provided, shall, before receiving the same, pay to [City Clerk,]* for the use of the city, the sum of ten dollars. Ten dollars to be paid for privilege.

SECT. 6. That so much of any ordinance as is inconsistent herewith be and the same is hereby repealed. Repealing clause.

Passed April 24th, 1851.

AN ORDINANCE

TO REGULATE THE PASSAGE OF CARS OVER THE RAILROADS IN THE CITY OF PHILADELPHIA.

SECT. 1. That all cars or trains of cars passing along the railroad in the city of Philadelphia, or along the railroad on the bridge at the end of High street, over the river Schuylkill, shall be drawn as herein set forth, namely: Passage of cars over the railroad in city regulated.

Every single loaded car, resting on a truck, having four wheels and no more, shall be drawn by at least one horse or two mules.

Every train of loaded cars resting upon trucks, having in the whole eight wheels, and no more, by at least three horses or three mules.

Every train of loaded cars resting upon trucks, having in the whole twelve wheels, and no more, by at least three horses or four mules.

---

*Chief Commissioner of Highways.

Every train of loaded cars, resting upon trucks having in the whole sixteen wheels, and no more, by at least four horses or six mules.

Every train of loaded cars, resting upon trucks having in the whole twenty wheels, and no more, by at least five horses or seven mules.

Every two trucks of eight wheels each, carrying section-boats, loaded or unloaded, by five horses or seven mules.

Every train of empty cars, resting upon trucks having twelve wheels, and no more, shall be drawn by at least two horses or three mules.

Every train of empty cars, resting upon trucks having twenty-four wheels, and no more, by three horses or five mules.

Every train of empty cars, resting upon trucks having thirty-two wheels, and no more, by four horses or six mules.

Every train of empty cars, resting upon trucks having forty wheels, and no more, by five horses or seven mules.

Penalty.

SECTION 2. That if any car or train of cars, or trucks carrying section-boats, shall be drawn on said railroads with a less number of horses or mules than is hereinbefore mentioned, the owner or owners, agent or agents, of every such car or truck, and the owner or owners, driver or drivers of such horses or mules, shall each be liable to forfeit and pay the sum of five dollars for each offence, which shall be sued for and recovered, in the manner that penalties for the violation of ordinances are by law sued for and recovered.

Passed February 6th, 1852.

A RESOLUTION

AUTHORIZING THE PENNSYLVANIA RAILROAD COMPANY TO REPAIR AND RELAY THE TRACK OF THE CITY RAILROAD, EAST OF EIGHTH STREET.

Co. may repair such parts of City R. R. track east of Eighth street as may be required.

Proviso.

Proviso.

Resolved, That the Pennsylvania Railroad Company be and they are hereby authorized to repair and relay such parts of the track of the city railroad, east of Eighth street, as may be required: *Provided,* The whole cost and expense of the same shall be deducted from the tolls accruing on said road, from sail Pennsylvania Railroad Company, up to July first, eighteen hundred and fifty-seven, agreeably to their proposition: *Provided*, That the city of Philadelphia shall not, in any event, be liable for any debt incurred for such repairs: *Provided*, That the relaying of the track and the repairs, shall be such as in the judgment of the Chief Engineer and Surveyor of the city shall be necessary, and that the same shall be done under his supervision. Proviso.

Adopted January 3d, 1856.

A RESOLUTION

AUTHORIZING THE MAYOR TO VOTE IN FAVOR OF APPROVAL OF THE PURCHASE OF THE MAIN LINE.

Resolved, That the Mayor of the city be and he is hereby authorized and requested to attend the approaching meeting of the stockholders of the Pennsylvania Railroad Company, and vote upon the shares of stock in said company, held by the city; to ratify and approve the purchase by the said company, of the main line of the public works of the State. Mayor authorized to vote for purchase of main line.

Approved July 3d, 1857.

AN ORDINANCE

TO AUTHORIZE THE WIDENING OF THE SPACE BETWEEN THE TRACKS IN THE CITY RAILROAD.

SECTION 1. That the Pennsylvania Railroad Company be and is hereby authorized to widen the space between the tracks of the city railroad, on Market street, east of Broad street, and at such points west of Broad street, as may be necessary to make the same conform to the space between the tracks of the said Pennsylvania Railroad; and that said company be allowed to withhold in payment of their tolls, one-half the cost of said alteration, or a sum equal to one-half: *Provided*, That the said alterations and repairs shall be made according to the plan, and agreeably to the directions of the Chief Engineer and Surveyor of Philadelphia. Company may widen space between tracks of City R. R. on Market street, to conform to their track, on certain terms. Proviso.

Approved December 22d, 1857.

ORDINANCES

OF THE

CITY OF PITTSBURGH.

AN ORDINANCE

GRANTING CERTAIN PRIVILEGES TO THE PENNSYLVANIA RAILROAD COMPANY.

Preamble.

WHEREAS, A convention of the citizens of Allegheny county, assembled on the 31st day of May, 1848, upon the call of the commissioners of said county, to advise with them on the propriety of subscribing to stock in the Pennsylvania Railroad Company: *and whereas*, The said convention did advise the said commissioners to subscribe for twenty thousand shares of said railroad stock: *And whereas*, The said county convention did advise the said county commissioners to impose a condition to said subscription, to wit: That the said company shall finally establish the terminus of their road within the limits of the city of Pittsburgh. *Therefore*, Fully acquiescing in the views of the convention as to the importance to the trade and prosperity of the city of Pittsburgh, that the terminus of said road should be located within its limits and at a point convenient for its shipping interests, and that every facility ought to be given to said company in the location and access to their depot, not only as it regards the convenient use of said road to the commercial and manufacturing interests, but in view of the fact that the city of Pittsburgh has become, by the act of the county commissioners, a partner and interested in the success and profit to be derived therefrom: *Therefore*,

Privilege to lay down rails through certain streets.

SECTION 1. That the right is hereby granted to the Pennsylvania Railroad Company to enter and lay down rails through the streets of said city, to wit: along Ferguson street to a convenient point, to curve into Liberty street, thence down Liberty street to the river, and that the said company shall have the privilege to traverse said streets with their cars and machinery: *Provided*, That after passing the curve aforesaid it shall not be competent for said company to exceed at any time a speed of four miles an hour, under such penalties as may hereafter be ordained and enacted by councils: *Provided, also*, That the said company shall at all times hereafter be subject to such rules and regulations as may be found necessary for the further protection and security of the persons and property of the citizens of said city.

Cars and machinery may pass.

Not to exceed four miles an hour.

Penalty.

Company to be subject to certain regulations.

SECTION 2. That for the construction of a depot to accommodate the trade of the city of Pittsburgh, upon and from said railroad, that there be granted, and the said authorities do hereby grant to the Pennsylvania Railroad Company, for so long as the said depot may be required by the said Pennsylvania Railroad Company, the use of sufficient ground on the levee or water front of the city, upon which the said company may construct the necessary buildings, beginning at the point opposite the corner of Liberty street, extending at right angles with Water street, thence to low water mark, and thence to the Allegheny river, at a rent of $3,000 per annum, or in the same proportion for any less quantity that the company may occupy and use, the rent to begin to accrue at and from the occupation of the building: *Provided*, That the said company shall cause Water street to be laid out at least sixty feet in width from the north side of said depot, and that the river side and ends of said depot shall be founded on piers, so that free access to said levee shall at all times be unobstructed by foundation walls, and kept open for public use, and that the right to have a passage at least thirty feet in width opposite Penn street, through and by which carriages, wagons, drays and other vehicles may have free access between said Penn street and the river, shall be reserved: *Provided, also*, That the occupancy of said ground by said company shall not interfere with the right of the officers of said city to collect wharfage on said levee, as though such depot had not been erected thereon: *Provided, also*, That the said company shall not at any time hereafter, either by themselves or their agents, engage in the business of forwarding merchants.

Ground for a depot granted.

Company may construct buildings.

Rent $3,000 per annum.

When rent to begin to accrue.

Water street to be sixty feet in width.

Passage of thirty feet opposite Penn street.

Wharfage to be collected by city officers.

Company not to be forwarding.

SECTION 3. That so much of any ordinance as is hereby altered or supplied, be and the same is hereby repealed.

Repealing clause.

ORDAINED AND ENACTED into a law in Councils this 15th day of June, A. D. 1848.

RECORDED July 10th, A. D. 1848, in Book A., p 406.

AN ORDINANCE

SUPPLEMENTARY TO "AN ORDINANCE GRANTING CERTAIN PRIVILEGES TO THE PENNSYLVANIA RAILROAD COMPANY," PASSED 15TH DAY OF JUNE, A. D. 1848.

Penna. R. R. Company.

WHEREAS, It has been discovered that an omission was made in transcribing the ordinance entitled "An ordinance granting certain privileges to the Pennsylvania Railroad Company," as recorded; therefore, *Be it ordained, &c.:*

Instructions to record the ordinance correctly.

SECTION 1. That the Clerks of Councils be, and they are hereby authorized and instructed, to have an ordinance entitled "An ordinance granting certain privileges to the Pennsylvania Railroad Company," passed the 16th day of June, A. D. 1848, correctly recorded, so that the latter clause of the second section may read as follows: "At a rent of three thousand dollars ($3,000) per annum for nine hundred feet, (900 feet) or in the same proportion for less quantity that the company may use."

ORDAINED AND ENACTED into a law in Councils this 5th day of January, A. D. 1849.

RECORDED January 24th, A. D. 1849, in Book A., p. 427.

AN ORDINANCE

GRANTING CERTAIN TEMPORARY PRIVILEGES TO THE PENNSYLVANIA RAILROAD COMPANY.

The privilege of laying track on West street and the wharf granted to Pa. R. R. Co.

SECTION 1. That the right is hereby granted to the Pennsylvania Railroad Company to enter on and lay down a track of rails through West street, from Liberty street to the Monongahela wharf, and from West street along said wharf to the western line of Ferry street; the said track not to be laid on Water street except where it enters from that street.

Permission given to Pa. R. R. Co. to erect a frame building on the wharf.

SECTION 2. Said company are hereby authorized to erect on said wharf a frame shed or building, which may extend from West street to the western line of Ferry street, and from Water street (60 feet in width) to low water mark; which shed is to be used for the reception and discharge of freight by steamboat or railroad, or other conveyances. *Provided*, That said company shall not engage in the forwarding business, and the privileges hereby granted shall not extend for a longer period than two years from the date of the passage of this ordinance. Proviso.

SECTION 3. Said company, for the privileges hereby granted, shall pay or cause to be paid into the treasury of the city, semi-annually, at the rate of three thousand dollars per annum, for 900 feet in length, (measured on the line of Water street,) or in the same proportion for any number of feet that the company may occupy within the prescribed limits, the rent to begin to accrue at and from the time of commencing the erection of the shed, and to terminate when all obstructions shall be removed from off said portions of the wharf; and the Pennsylvania Railroad Company are to leave West street, Water street, and the Monongahela wharf in as good repair as at the passage of this ordinance. Conditions.

SECTION 4. Said shed or building shall be exempt from the penalties and provisions of the ordinances relating to frame buildings. The right of the city to collect wharfage in front of said shed or building shall not be impaired by anything herein contained. Building to be exempt from the usual penalties and provisions.

ORDAINED AND ENACTED into a law in Councils this 8th day of September, A. D. 1852.

AN ORDINANCE

FOR VACATING PARTS OF EIGHTH STREET AND PLUMB ALLEY, AND SURRENDERING THE SAME TO THE PENNSYLVANIA RAILROAD COMPANY.

SECTION 1. That one hundred feet of Eighth street, and one hundred feet of Plumb alley, running from Grant street, be vacated and surrendered to the Pennsylvania Railroad Company on the following conditions: Parts of Eighth st. and Plumb alley surrendered to Pennsylvania Railroad Co.

1st. That the same shall be used and occupied for the purposes of an inner passenger depot and station, and not otherwise.

2d. That the said railroad company will take down and remove all the present buildings on the triangular lot, No. —, and will not erect any house thereon, and surrender to the city the control of the same.

Company to lay out alley. 3d. That the said company will lay out, on their own ground, an alley twenty feet wide, extending from Seventh to Eighth street, which shall be used by the public, except upon the arrival or departure of railroad cars, when it may be necessary temporarily to close the same for the purpose of avoiding any hindrance and interruption to their business.

ORDAINED AND ENACTED into a law in Councils this 27th day of September, A. D. 1852.

AN ORDINANCE

RELATIVE TO THE VACATION OF CERTAIN STREETS IN THE NINTH WARD.

Preamble. WHEREAS, By the third section of an act of assembly passed the 23d day of April, A. D. 1852, entitled "A further supplement to an act to incorporate the Pennsylvania Railroad Company, Eighth street and Plumb alley, in the city of Pittsburgh, and all other streets extending through the property of said company, are vacated, and the title thereto vested in the said company; *Provided*, The Councils of said city give their assent thereto. And whereas, the Pennsylvania Railroad Company has applied for the assent of the Councils to the vacation of certain streets in the Ninth Ward of said city, extending through the depot or ground of said company;

Vacation of certain streets. *Be it ordained and enacted by the Select and Common Councils of the city of Pittsburgh, and it is hereby enacted by the authority of the same*, That the assent of the Councils be and it is hereby given to the vacation of so much of Carroll, Wilkins, Baldwin, Morris and Rush streets, and Sassafras alley, as extend through the grounds, or is held or used by said company, and so much of Furguson street as lies between a point on said street 550 feet east from the eastern line of Lumber street and Morton street, so long as the Pennsylvania Railroad Company use the same for railroad purposes; *Provided*, That no injury shall be done to the interests of the Western Pennsylvania Hospital; and provided, that the said company shall, at its own cost, when the public convenience may require it, at the

Proviso.

request and under the direction of Councils, cause to be laid out and graded along the south line of the southern track of said railroad, and parallel to and adjoining therewith, a space or street of forty feet in width, extending the length of that part of Furguson street vacated and connecting therewith.

ORDAINED AND ENACTED into a law in Councils this twenty-eighth day of July, A. D. 1853.

RECORDED August 16, 1853, in Ordinance Book, vol. 2, p. 16.

AN ORDINANCE

TO PROVIDE FOR THE REGULATION OF TURN-OUTS, SWITCHES, &c., FROM ANY RAILROAD WITHIN THE LIMITS OF THE CITY.

SECTION 1. *Be it ordained and enacted by the citizens of Pittsburgh, in Select and Common Councils assembled*, That from and after the passage of this ordinance, the Mayor of the city of Pittsburgh, in connection with and with the consent of the Committee on Streets, be and he is hereby authorized to grant a license or permission to any person or persons, company or companies, owning or occupying property situated upon the streets or alleys through which any railroads, entering or passing through the city, may be laid, to attach turn-outs, bolting tracks, or switches to the main tracks thereof; the consent of the railroad company being first obtained; said turn-outs, bolting tracks or switches to be laid down in such manner as to conform to the established heights and level of the streets or alleys in which they may be placed; and such licenses or permission shall be in writing, and shall be subject to the provisions of this and other ordinances relating to railroads, turn-outs, or other fixtures in the city of Pittsburgh, which have or may hereafter be enacted; *Provided* such license or permission shall not be granted for a longer term than one year, and that no license or permission shall be granted for a less period than six months; *And provided further*, That no turn-out, bolting track, switch or other fixtures shall be permitted to extend beyond the property owned or occupied by the person or persons, company or companies, applying therefor, and situated and fronting on the line

Permission to build switches, &c., granted.

Proviso.

of the street or alley on which the railroad is constructed, with which said turn-out, bolting track, switch or other fixture is to connect; *And provided also*, That this ordinance shall not be construed to conflict in any manner with the right of any railroad company to regulate and control any turn-out, bolting track, switch, or other fixture which may be constructed or laid down in pursuance of this ordinance.

SECTION 2. That it shall and may be lawful for the Committee on Streets, from time to time, to establish and put in force such rules, regulations and restrictions in relation to such turn-outs, bolting tracks or switches, their construction and materials, and the repairing thereof, as to the said committee shall seem fit and proper, and no turn-out, bolting track, switch or other fixture shall be attached to the said railroads, or laid over, on any street or alley, or be considered as repaired, unless the same shall conform in every particular to the rules and regulatious so adopted.

Duty of Street Committee.

SECTION 3. That all such turn-outs, bolting tracks, switches or other fixtures shall be laid down or repaired under the direction of said Committee on Streets, together with the Street Commissioner of the district in which the same is situated, and if any person or persons, company or companies shall construct, lay down or repair any turn-outs, bolting tracks, switch or other fixture contrary to the provisions of this ordinance or of any ordinance relative thereto, which may be hereafter enacted, or of any regulation adopted by the Committee on Streets, the person or persons, company or companies so offending shall forfeit and pay the sum of seventy-five dollars, to be sued for and recovered in the manner that penalties for the breach of ordinances are by law recoverable, and in addition thereto, such turn-out, bolting track, switch or other fixture shall be forthwith removed.

Penalty.

SECTION 4. That if any turn-out, bolting track, switch, turning platform, or other fixture shall be out of order and repair, and the owner or person having charge thereof shall refuse or neglect to repair, or put the same in good order, after five days' notice from the Street Commissioner of the district, the same shall be taken up and removed under the direction of the Committee on Streets together with the Street Commissioner of the district, and the owner or person having charge of such turn-out, bolting track, switch, turning platform or other fixture, shall also forfeit and pay the sum of twenty-five dollars, and all necessary repairs and expenses incident to removal, to be sued for and recovered in the manner that penalties for the breach of city ordinances are by law recoverable. *Pro-*

Penalty.

vided, That the turn-out, bolting track, switch, turning platform or fixture after being so removed, shall not be replaced unless by permission or license of the Mayor of the city and Committee on streets, nor until all the expenses of such removal shall first be paid. Proviso.

SECTION 5. That the person or persons, company or companies to whom license or permission may be granted to attach any turn-out, bolting track, or any other fixture to any railroad within the limits of the city, as hereinbefore provided, shall before obtaining the same pay to the Mayor, for the use of the city, such tax, rent, or assessment as may be agreed upon by the Mayor and Committee on Streets: *Provided*, That the same be not less than twenty-five, nor more than two hundred dollars. License.

SECTION 6. That it shall not be lawful for any person or persons, company or companies, to obstruct any street or alley in the city by loading or unloading, placing, keeping, or cause to be placed or kept any car or other vehicle on any part of any turn-out, bolting track or switch, which may be laid down or constructed in pursuance of this ordinance, or any ordinance relative thereto which may hereafter be passed; but all cars or other vehicles must be loaded or unloaded, placed, kept, or caused to be placed or kept on the ground owned or occupied by the person or persons having the license or permission to lay down such turn-out, bolting track, switch or other fixture. Any person or persons, company or companies, violating the provisions of this section of this ordinance, shall be liable to the penalty of five dollars for every such violation, to be recovered in the manner hereinbefore mentioned. Penalty.

SECTION 7. That in all cases where turn-outs, bolting tracks, or other fixtures attached to or connected with the main track of the Pennsylvania Railroad within the limits of this city having been constructed by private individuals prior to the passage of this ordinance, it shall be the duty of the Street Commissioner of the proper district to notify the person or persons owning or using the same, to take out a license or permission therefor, and in case the person or persons owning or using such turn-out, bolting track, switch or other fixture, shall neglect or refuse to take out such license or permission within ten days from the time of receiving such notice, he or they so neglecting or refusing shall be liable to a penalty of seventy-five dollars, to be recovered in the manner hereinbefore mentioned; and in addition thereto, such turn-out, bolting track, or other fixture, shall be forthwith taken up and removed under the direction of the Committee on Streets together with the Street Commissioner of Penalty.

the proper district, and no license or permission shall be granted to replace the same until all the expenses of such removal are first paid.

ORDAINED AND ENACTED into a law in Councils this seventeenth day of September, A. D. 1853.

RECORDED September 28, 1853, in Ordinance Book, vol. 2, p. 17.

AN ORDINANCE

RELATING TO CERTAIN STREETS IN THE NINTH WARD.

Preamble.

WHEREAS, The interests of the Western Pennsylvania Hospital have sustained a serious injury from the obstructions occasioned by the stoppage of the locomotives and cars belonging to the Pennsylvania Railroad, on Ferguson street, at the intersection of Morton street; and

Preamble.

WHEREAS, Public convenience requires that the Pennsylvania Railroad Company should forthwith proceed to lay out and grade the street parallel with Ferguson street, provided for in the ordinance of 28th July, 1853, relative to the vacation of certain streets in the Ninth Ward of this city: Therefore,

R. R. Co. not to obstruct Ferguson street.

SECTION 1. *Be it ordained and enacted by the Select and Common Councils of the City of Pittsburgh,* That from and after the passage of this ordinance, it shall not be lawful for said Pennsylvania Railroad Company, or its officers, agents, or employees, to obstruct the passage across Ferguson street, at its intersection with Morton street, by the stoppage or detention of any locomotive, tender, or car on such portion of Ferguson street aforesaid, as lies between the eastern and western lines of Morton street.

R. R. Co. to extend Ferguson street.

SECTION 2. *Be it ordained, &c.,* That the said Pennsylvania Railroad Company be, and they are hereby requested to lay out and grade along the south line of the southern track of said railroad, and parallel to, and adjoining therewith, a street of forty feet in width, extending the length of that part of Ferguson street, provisionally vacated by the said ordinance of the 28th July, 1858; and the said company is hereby directed to have the said street laid out and opened within six months after the passage of this ordinance, under the supervision of the Street Regulator and Committee on Streets.

SECTION 3. *Be it ordained, &c.*, That, in case the said Pennsylvania Railroad Company shall refuse or neglect to comply with the provisions of this ordinance, according to the true intent and meaning thereof, such failure or neglect shall be considered as a violation on the part of said company of the provisions of said ordinance of 28th July, 1853, and shall subject the said company to a forfeiture of all the rights and privileges granted by said ordinance.

Penalty of neglect.

ORDAINED AND ENACTED into a law in Councils this 7th day of February, A. D. 1854.

RECORDED March 6th, A. D. 1854.

AN ORDINANCE

RELATIVE TO THE VACATION OF BELL'S ALLEY.

SECTION 1. That "Bell's Alley," from Liberty street to Exchange alley, be and the same is hereby vacated, and the use of the ground occupied by the same be and is hereby granted to the Pennsylvania Railroad: *Provided*, said company pay the city for said property, at the same rate they have paid for adjoining property, to wit: $150 per foot front: *Provided*, That whenever the said ground shall cease to be used for the purpose of a depot, the same shall revert to the city. That the said company shall be allowed to construct, not to exceed three curves from their track on Liberty street, at any convenient point or points, into any part of either of their depots: *Provided*, That the street and pavement be not obstructed, and the work be done under the supervision of the Street Committee, with stone, in a permanent manner.

Bell's Alley to be vacated for the use of R. R. Company.

SECTION 2. That all curves, sidings or switches, now or hereafter constructed by companies or individuals, brought into depot, warehouse, or any other place from the main track, shall be constructed in a substantial and permanent manner with stone, so as not to obstruct the street or pavement, under the supervision of the Street Committee.

Construction of sidings, &c.

ORDAINED AND ENACTED into a law in Councils this 9th day of May, A. D. 1854.

RECORDED June 8th, A. D. 1854.

AN ORDINANCE

FIXING A PENALTY FOR RUNNING CARS AND MACHINERY ON LIBERTY STREET AT A GREATER SPEED THAN FOUR MILES AN HOUR.

Preamble.

WHEREAS, By section first of an ordinance, entitled "An ordinance, granting certain privileges to the Pennsylvania Railroad Company," it is provided, that after passing the curve aforesaid it shall not be competent for said company to exceed, at any time, a speed of four miles an hour, under such penalties as may hereafter be ordained and enacted by Councils. *And whereas*, It is believed that the cars and machinery of said Pennsylvania Railroad do exceed the rate of four miles an hour on Liberty street, within the city limits. Therefore, *Be it ordained, &c.*

Company not to exceed certain rate of speed on Liberty street, under certain penalty.

SECTION 1. That it shall be unlawful for the cars and machinery of said Pennsylvania Railroad Company to exceed the rate of four miles per hour on Liberty street, under a penalty of not less than fifty, nor more than one hundred dollars, for each and every offence, to be recovered, with costs, by any person who shall sue for the same, before the mayor or any alderman of the city, in the same manner as other penalties are now by law recoverable, one half of the penalty to go to informer, the other half to the city.

Repeal.

SECTION 4. That all ordinances and parts of ordinances inconsistent herewith, be and the same are hereby repealed.

ORDAINED AND ENACTED into a law in Councils, this 29th day of December, 1856.

RECORDED January 9th, A. D. 1857, in Book vol. 2, p. 68.

ORDINANCE AND RESOLUTION

OF THE

BOROUGH OF HARRISBURG.

The following ordinance in relation to the running of locomotives and cars within the limits of the Borough of Harrisburg was adopted:

WHEREAS, it is represented by the owners and occupiers of real property, residing along Meadow lane, Mulberry and Canal streets, and also by farmers and strangers visiting our borough, that they are greatly aggrieved and annoyed by reason of locomotive engines and cars running at a rate not less than twenty miles to the hour, and not giving due notice when passing main streets, thereby endangering the lives and property of individuals; Therefore, *Be it ordained by the Town Council of the Borough of Harrisburg*, That no locomotive engine, with or without cars attached thereto, or cars without motive power of any description shall be suffered by the engineer or conductor thereof, to run at a greater speed than four miles an hour, within the limits of the borough; and any engineer or other person guilty of a violation of this ordinance, shall be fined in the sum of ten dollars for the first offence and fifteen dollars for the second, which fine shall be sued for and recovered before the Chief or Assistant Burgess, as debts of like amount are now by law recoverable, the one half for the use of the borough and the other half for the use of the informer, and in no case shall the fine be remitted, unless with the consent of the Council. Preamble. Speed of locomotives in borough limits. Penalty.

SECT. 2. All former ordinances on this subject, so far as the same are hereby altered or amended, are hereby repealed. Repeal.

Passed May 3d, 1851.

The following preamble and resolution was adopted:

WHEREAS, The Harrisburg and Lancaster Railroad Company propose to build a large and spacious depot on the site of the present one, extending to Chestnut street; and to enable said company to locate and erect the building in such manner as to afford reasonable accommodation to the various railroads centering at this place, and to meet the requirements of the public, they have requested permission of the Town Council to occupy and lay tracks on Meadow lane, adjoining the railroad between Market and Chesnut streets;

Depot allowed to be built.

Therefore, Resolved, that the request of the said company be and is hereby granted on the following terms and conditions, viz: That no part of said street or lane now asked for shall be used as a new siding on which to stand cars, but as and for a through track; and provided that the railroad track or tracks shall be so laid and put down as not to obstruct or interfere with the ordinary use of said lane by the public, when not occupied by the business of the railroad company, and that the Street Committee of the South Ward is hereby instructed to attend to and see that this preamble and resolution is properly carried out."

On what conditions.

Passed September 1st, 1855.

ORDINANCE

OF THE BOROUGH OF ALTOONA.

Company may lay down water pipes in any of the streets or alleys of the borough.

That the right is hereby granted to the Pennsylvania Railroad Company to lay down water pipes in any of the streets or alleys of the borough of Altoona, including the Greensburg extensions, and to adopt from time to time such measures and to do all things convenient and necessary for examining the condition of said water pipes, and keeping the same in good order and repair. *Provided*, that the said Pennsylvania Railroad Company shall be responsible for any damages that may accrue from laying of said water pipes, and provided further, that in laying down or examining and repairing said water pipes, the streets or alleys shall not be obstructed, or the ditch for pipes be kept open longer at any one time than is really necessary for the completion of said work.

Proviso.

Proviso.

Passed May 12, 1858.

BY-LAWS

OF THE

PENNSYLVANIA RAILROAD COMPANY,

AS REVISED AND APPROVED BY THE BOARD OF DIRECTORS

SEPTEMBER 17, 1856.

BY-LAWS.

Section I.

The Stated Meetings of the Board shall be held in Philadelphia, on every other Wednesday, unless otherwise ordered, at such place and hour as they may from time to time designate, and *Special Meetings* may be called by the President whenever he may deem it necessary, or at the request of any three members, in writing. Seven members shall constitute a quorum for the transaction of business.

Stated meetings. Special meetings. Quorum.

Section II.

The President shall preside at all meetings of the Board, or in his absence the Vice President, preserve order and regulate debate according to the usual parliamentary rules. He shall have the custody of the seal of the Company, conduct the correspondence, and attend generally to the executive business of the Company, under the direction of the Board. In the absence of the President and Vice President, a President *pro tem.* shall be appointed by the Board.

The President.

Section III.

The Treasurer shall give bonds, with one or more sureties, (not members of the Board,) in the sum of fifty thousand dollars, for the faithful performance of all his duties, as recited in the sixth section of the act of incorporation. He shall keep a regular set of books containing the accounts of the company, and all its funds that may pass through his hands, and keep a separate account, as Treasurer, in such bank or banks as the Board of Directors may from time to time designate. He shall, on the Monday preceding the first stated meeting of the Board in each month, submit to the Chairman of the Finance Committee, to be by him laid before the

The Treasurer.

Board at the next stated meeting thereafter, a statement of the financial condition of the Company as it stood on the last day of the preceding month; and at the second stated meeting in January of each year, he shall present to the Board a complete statement of his accounts, for the year ending on the last day of December of the previous year, as required of the Board of Directors by section 19 of the act of incorporation, and section 2 of the supplement of April 26, 1850; and shall attend to such other duties connected with the finances of the Company, as may be required by the Board. His books shall at all times be open to the inspection of the President, or any member of the Board. All checks shall be signed by the Treasurer. All office bills and petty expenses of the general office at Philadelphia, shall be paid by orders drawn upon the Treasurer by direction of the Board, and signed by the Secretary.

All other bills shall, before being paid, be examined and approved by the Auditor, whose approval shall be endorsed thereon.

All bonds, mortgages, and other securities of the Company, shall be placed in charge of the Treasurer.

Section IV.

The Secretary. *The Secretary* shall keep a regular record of the proceedings of the Board, give notice to the members of all stated and special meetings, and attend the meetings of all standing or special committees when required.

He shall cancel old certificates at the time of transfer, and shall register all certificates of stock that are issued, and sign the same, and in his absence the Vice President will attend to this part of his duties.

He shall issue orders on the Treasurer, for office bills and petty expenses of office, as the Board may from time to time direct by resolution.

He shall give twenty days' notice of the *Annual*, and ten days' notice of other *General* or *Special Meetings* of the Stockholders, as required by section 4 of theact of incorporation; and attend to such other duties as the President or Board of Directors may require.

Section V.

Office of the company, when open. *The Office* of the Company shall be in Philadelphia, and kept open every day except Sundays, Christmas, and Fourth of July, between the hours of nine and three o'clock, unless otherwise ordered by the Board.

SECTION VI.

A Solicitor at Philadelphia, shall be elected annually, at the first stated meeting in April, whose duty it shall be to give advice and opinion on such subjects as may be referred to him, and shall attend to such legal business of the Company at Philadelphia, or elsewhere, as the President or Board of Directors may require. Solicitor.

SECTION VII.

The administrative duties of the business of the Company will be divided among the four following departments:

The Transportation Department,

Having charge of the road and its management.

The Auditor's Department,

Having charge of all accounts and settlements.

The Legal Department,

Having charge of the legal and such other business pertaining thereto, as may be required by the President or Board of Directors, on the line of the Pennsylvania Railroad, excepting in Dauphin county.

The Treasury Department,

Having charge of all payments and receipts of money. Each department, with the exception of the legal department, to be conducted by one officer having the direction and responsibility of the business thereof, and the whole to be under the general direction of the President, as the organ of the Board of Directors.

SECTION VIII.

Certificates of Stock shall be issued to the stockholders, and transfers of them shall be made when required; said certificates to be signed by the President, countersigned by the treasurer, authenticated by the seal of the company, in accordance with the provisions of the act of incorporation, and signed by the register and transfer clerk. And any person or persons claiming a certificate or evidence of stock to be issued in lieu of one lost or destroyed, shall make an affidavit or affirmation of the fact; shall advertise the same in one or more newspapers in Philadelphia, twice a week for four weeks, describing the certificate, and shall transmit the affidavit or Certificates of stock.

affirmation, with the advertisement, and shall give the board a bond of indemnity, with one or more securities, if required, in double the sum of money paid on such certificate to be renewed, against any damage that may arise from the issuing of a new certificate. Whereupon the president and treasurer may, one month after the last advertisement, issue a new certificate of the same tenor with the one alleged to be lost or destroyed, therein specifying that it is in lieu thereof. Old certificates shall be canceled as is provided in the 4th section of these by-laws.

Section IX.

Committees. There shall be appointed annually, at the first stated meeting after the organization of the board in March, a Standing Committee on Finance, and a Standing Committe on the Road, to consist of five members each, and a Standing Committee on Accounts, to consist of three members. The Committee on Finance shall have a general supervision of the finances of the company, and report their proceedings to the board at the first stated meeting of every month, or oftener if required, and shall invest the funds of the company agreeably to the provisions of the charter, under the direction of the board. The Committee on the Road shall have a general oversight of all matters connected with the construction and management of the road and its appurtenances. There shall be added to this committee, at the first stated meeting in every month, another member of the board, for the month, so that the directors may thus serve monthly in rotation.

It shall be the duty of the Committee on Accounts to examine and audit all office bills before being presented to the board for payment, and to have a general supervision of the accounts of the treasurer.

Besides these, the President and Vice President shall be *ex officio* members of all committees, and to each of the standing committees shall be added one of the directors from the county of Allegheny.

Each standing committee shall keep a regular record of its proceedings.

Section X.

Elections. *All elections* for officers shall be by ballot, unless by unanimous consent, when the vote may be taken *viva voce.* All committees shall be appointed by the president, unless otherwise ordered by the board.

Section XI.

No member of the board, or any officer or agent by them appointed, shall be directly or indirectly concerned in any contract, arrangement, or engagement for doing any work, or furnishing any materials, or in any way be interested whereby any profit or advantage may come to him or them in relation to the construction of the road, or any part of it. No member, officer or agent, to be interested in contracts.

Section XII.

The Order of Business shall be as follows: Order of Business.

1. When a quorum appears, viz., seven directors, the President shall call the board to order.
2. The minutes shall be read, and considered as approved if there be no motion to amend.
3. Reports of committees.
4. Reports of officers of the company.
5. Miscellaneous communications.
6. Unfinished business.
7. New business.

Section XIII.

No alteration or amendment shall be made in these *By-Laws*, unless presented at a stated meeting and considered at a subsequent stated meeting, but any By-Law may be suspended by the consent of not less than two-thirds of the *whole* board. Alteration or amendment of by-laws.

GENERAL INDEX.

A.

B.

C.

D.

E.

G.

H.

I.

J.

L.

M.

N.

O.

P.

Q.

R.

S.

T.

U.

V.

W.

Y.

CPSIA information can be obtained
at www.ICGtesting.com
Printed in the USA
LVHW100750250223
740366LV00007B/533

9 783382 307349